The Misadventures of

Pinocchio

a libretto by

Michael Charles Tobias

Zorba Press
http://www.ZorbaPress.com

Published by Zorba Press
http://www.ZorbaPress.com

For more information, contact Zorba Press by email:
zorbapress AT gmail.com

The Misadventures of Pinocchio (libretto)
Paperback edition 2012 October 01

ISBN: 9780927379267

Printings
0102030405060708091011121214151617181920

The Misadventures of Pinocchio

A Libretto/Singspiel, based upon the legendary novel, Le avventure di Pinocchio — Storia di un Burattino, by Carlo Collodi (pseudonimo dello scrittore Carlo Lorenzini a Firenze con le illustrazioni di Enrico Mazzanti), and published in 1883 in Florence under the auspices and authority of Felice Paggi Libraio-Editore.

Act 1
Scene 1

The interior of a rustic hut sitting squarely in the center of a hamlet in the hills overlooking the sea. Early winter. A cold wind blows in the last of Autumn's colorful leaves. The old man, Geppetto has just arrived home carrying a large piece of wood in a gunnysack, which he drops onto the floor in the middle of his workshop. A clamber of chimes as the wind rushes all about his magically intimate interior.

A medley of flamboyant Marionettes – all human-sized, and human more or less, but comically so, puppets full-grown, clowns both strange and otherwordly – stop their merrymaking adjoining the fireplace in Geppetto's little house, which is adorned sparsely, with tools of his wood-cutting trade all about, a few baguettes of bread, some bottles of wine, a few tattered posters and newspaper clippings on the wall, as well as some other memorabilia of his life and a single picture, hanged crookedly, a glossy poster copy of the 19th century Macchiaioli impressionist landscapist, the Luccan, Roberto Pasquinelli, of some typical Italian Arcady.

The hut in which Geppetto lives looks out upon the forest, a village square, and beyond – mountains, horizon and sea, that same precious landscape as in the painting. Chimes seem to be hanging every which way, as there are tools, a work table, a little dinner table of solid dark oak, and various costumes, masques, and other paraphernalia of the Marionettes. It is a festive scene, if surreal.

Now, a strange primitive yelp from the gunnysack on the floor, which starts to move about. All the Marionettes – weirdly lit as in some Hyderabad or Javanese (oil shadows staging) – crowd round to get a better view of the new arrival.

> Geppetto
> Sono confuso improvvisamente?
> What *is* that?

From the sack he has emptied on the floor, a thing wrestling to get out. Everyone jumps back,
terrified.
Finally, the blunt large wooden mass rolls forth,
like unformed clay.

Geppetto
Neither squirrel nor rat. Un certo
genere di *mostro!* Yes, definitely a
monster, God help me!

Marionettes
Yes, a MOSTRO MOSTRO!

The wood twists and turns, groaning hoarsely, like
a primeval hamadryad, Geppetto leaping back,
falling onto the floor, pulling himself away in fright.

Geppetto
Definitely a demon! Signore mi salva
dal *gunnysack!*. Sia bandito di
demone!

Geppetto then reaches for his axe as if to lunge
and kill the demonic creature.

Geppetto
Cosa orribile. Cosa di Monstous!

But the wood begins to screech hysterically,
lurching away in fear.

> Geppetto (stepping close to the
> "creature")
> And what's more, a clever demon, on
> the attack!

The wood is now behaving like a Mexican jumping
bean, exploring the finitude of its wooden exterior,
and uttering a bizarre vocal range we've never
heard before. As if a Shaku-Haji Japanese flute, in
tune with a Didgeridoo trance dance were sung by
a humming bird in concert with a whale, in slow-
motion and in reverse.

All the Marionettes whisper and confer (in garbled
chatter) — "What if it's a bomb? Grey Wolves?
PKK terrorists? A trick by the Mafia?

> Geppetto
> Or just wood with a chip on its
> shoulder?

> Marionettes
> Ha-ha-ha!

> Piece of Wood
> The wood starts crying.

Marionettes
What is that? (they come nearer)
That sounds like it's crying?

Geppetto
Nonsense. (And he raises his axe
ever more menacingly)

Suddenly the piece of wood cries out,
"C'era una volta un pezzo di legno!"

Geppetto
What? Can't be.

Marionettes
Impossible! Copycat!

Geppetto (to the piece of wood)
What did you say?

Piece of Wood (turning to address
Geppetto and all his Marionettes)
I, I don't know. It's the only Italian I
ever heard.

Geppetto

But that's ... that's by somebody,
what's his name? Shit, we all grew
up hearing it. I just can't put my
finger on it.

Piece of Wood

Yes, yes! It was definitely a somebody. My parents used to sing his
praises. And hoped that someday I
might also grow up in a similar
manner. I have no idea what they
meant. But the minute his name was
uttered, all the forests came to life,
as if a fresh summer wind had
moved through. That's all I know.

Geppetto

You are no ordinary piece of wood,
that much can be declared for
certain.

Piece of Wood

Please, good Sir, don't harm me.

Geppetto
Why don't you speak Italian? This IS
Italy?

Marionettes
When in Rome —

Piece of Wood
My Italian suffers from having been
wooden for so long. Anyway, my
parents always had a translator
nearby.

Geppetto
Translator?   What are you talking
about? Parents? ... Translators? ...
(To the Marionettes —) I traduttori,
immaginano quello! Ciò è assurdità.
You're just a piece of wood.

Piece of Wood
I can't explain. I'm no traduttori, as
you say.

Geppetto
Not traduttori, but traduttore. It's what

they call in school, the singular my
little friend.

Piece of Wood
I've never been to school. I'd like to
though. But English is my only
tongue, forgive me!

Marionettes (starting to get the
heebee jeebies)
Don't, don't you dare forgive him,
Geppetto. You never forgave us just
for merely sampling your red wine.
Not a sip of vino since. You've
deprived us of drink for nine whole
years to the day.

One of them whispers – "Bastard!"

Geppetto
A sample you say? Why, you drank
through my entire stash, ten year's
worth in one night. You left nothing.

Marionettes
That's not so. We left the bottles.

They're worth something at the
recycling center down the block, no?

Geppetto
We didn't recycle then, except for a
newspaper or two. You know that?
Anyway, even a poor woodcutter like
Geppetto is entitled to a little red
wine after an exhausting day in the
forest, only to be swindled, cheated,
and made a gasping fool of by you
Marionettes who've hardly ever
made a Lire out in the theatre, which
was our deal, remember?. I don't
care if you are direct descendants of
whoever the hell you claim to be.

Tallest Marionette
That would be Victor Immanuel the
Second himself, a true sardine who
hired our grandparents to help shoot
off fireworks to commemorate the
merging of two Sesamies and seven
Italian steaks.

All the Marionettes slap their hearts with their right

hands shouting, "Saluté Girabaldi, God Bless Mazzini!"

Geppetto
That's Sicilies not sesamies you dim wit! And states, not steaks, morons! And I'll have you know that MY grandfather built a carriage for Count Cajillo Benso di Cavour –

Marionettes
Yeah yeah yeah, You've told us – (in unison) Chief Minister of Victor Emmanuel.

Geppetto
And he was, too. The true architect of Italian reunification.

Marionettes
Listen to that! You'd think he was some learned type fellow, speaking like that.

Piece of Wood
He sounds pretty learned to me.

Geppetto
You're damn straight, kid.

Marionettes (among one another)
Now he's calling that dumb clump of
wood `kid'. At this rate he'll be
offering him buttered bread and us,
just the crumbs! I don't like it. I'm
saying it now, I sense ill-boding
omens.

Geppetto (putting down his axe and
scratching his grey beard)
I must confess, I am not a little
perplexed by this audacious piece of
wood. It is like nothing I've ever
seen, be it Sardinia, Piedmont or
Savoy.
Still, he's just a fine piece of wood
and he'll make a wonderful fire to
keep out the chill.

Geppetto prepares to chop the little creature in half
with his axe. When –

Piece of Wood
For heaven's sake, stop! For I am a wonderful piece of wood, you said it yourself.

Geppetto
No, I said you'd make for a wonderful fire.

Piece of Wood
There's more to me than just another fire. How many fires have there been throughout time?

Marionettes
It's a trick question.

Geppetto
Plenty. Especially if you include wildfires. Boy, you really do know your English.

Piece of Wood
Of course. It is the language of Shakespeare!

Marionettes
Did you hear that? A piece of wood
familiar with Shakespeare. Next the
little demon will be trying to quote
Dante! Roberto Benigni.
The Tiniest of the Marionettes
Not to mention Capollini and Fussili!
Which reminds me, not only no wine,
I haven't eaten in years!

Piece of Wood
From a tree that rose to the heavens
with higher hopes than wood chips
for your senseless fire, pointless pulp
or toilet paper; And for hundreds of
years soaked in the rain, conversed
with the wind, gobbled up sunbeams,
basked in blue skies, survived
droughts and bark beetles, one blight
after another, and gloried to good
earth below. An axe would truly be
just terribly unkind, and surely not the
happiest of endings for so pure a
dream as mine, wouldn't you agree?

Geppetto (stunned, kneeling down,
lowering his axe)
But where is your mouth to shape
such dreams and things? What
branches, roots, or saplings have
ever had audacity like this to
challenge the logic of a hearth? Or
condemn the survival instinct that
wishes only to be warm, provide a
family with its needs, when Winter
such as ours proves ruthless, brute
icicles all around, frozen boots,
hands chilled to the bone, and no
prayer to warm the waning heart.

Piece of wood
I, too, have cares, and my parents
said I was heartwood through and
through, immune to decomposition,
unlike my siblings, all sapwoods.

Geppetto
Heartwood? Well, you are darker, it's
true. And I detect some grain,
compression, that, on your head, a
knot whose breaking strength I'll

wager is right up there.

Piece of Wood
I grew up beside a willow and a
poplar, down the ridge some hickory,
black locust and something my Uncle
said was twenty percent
hemicellulose.

Marionettes
Holy shit! A friggin genius, as pieces
of wood go! Damn! What's
hemicellulose?

Geppetto
You're a conifer.

Piece of Wood
More complex.

Geppetto
Mulberry?

Piece of Wood
My grandmother dated a mulberry.
But I am no mulberry.

Geppetto

I know what you are. You are a pine,
a pine nut, precisely. I cut a pine with
a single blow, I know a pine when I
see one. And you, young man, are a
pine that's becoming a pain. No more
arguments.

Marionettes

First a kid, now Geppetto is calling
him a young man. This isn't
happening. He never called me a
young man. Dumb-head, yes. Young
man? Never. We're losing the battle.
As it is, he hangs us up on hooks
every night.

Piece of Wood

Yes. Pine is fine. I conduct water,
produce fiber as soft as silk and my
porosity is just one side of my
precocity.

Marionette

A poet no less. Shit. We're screwed.
Geppetto's falling for it. This stinky

hut was never big enough for all of
us in the first place. And now this
arrogant little prick fresh out of the
forest.

Piece of Wood
I beg your pardon, puppets? All I'm
saying is, I'll not be hewn without a
plan; nor dumbly cleft and shattered
for purposes of your indifferent clan
that craves a primitive fire, but at the
expense of a soul that fully aspires.

Geppetto
Who are you then? If not a dumb
chunk of pine pining for some other
place in the hierarchy of places?

Piece of Wood
Loved, admired, sculpted like true
Michelangelo!

Geppetto (turning to the Marionettes,
contemplating this new and
astonishing situation)
Hewn, sculpted you say? Invoking

Michelangelo, the artist I assume.
And words infrequently used these
days. Next he'll invoke three coins in
a fountain, Bernini, even the Pope!
Did I wake up this morning? Is this a
strange dream?

Piece of Wood
And a forest rarely seen, my
birthplace. Stars above, leaves and
fallen flowers below. The place has
no other address than wilderness. It
is no dream. It is your birthright.
Yours, mine, all of us. We were born
in the forest, I might remind you.

Geppetto
Yes. The forest is my home. But
never have I encountered so blunt
and expressive a piece of wood as
you. Occasionally there is the odd
face in a tree, or so it seems. Knobs,
knots, pine-shillings, the Great
Carbuncle out of which I might make
myself a pipe from Argentine elm, a
pair of clunker shoes from Siberian

ash, shoes, pipe, but never poesy.
Nor has a puppet with such
perplexing pedigree ever shown true
colors in this wood. (To the
Marionettes –) Would you not agree?

Marionettes
Never. Never. No how. No way. A
piece of wood who thinks himself a
He, a Him, an It. Why t'is nothing but
an imposter, and totally unfit. Clad
dumbly in the fir of forest, not a
puppet's brain, and certainly not the
human flesh it mimics with disdain.
Give him the licking he deserves,
saw him left, saw him right, but do
not let him mock you without a fight.
Make him a flame for all time!

Piece of Wood
I'm not impressed by a jealous mob
of Marionettes that try to rhyme. I've
heard better day and night and night
and day for centuries or more. The
forest has said it all before. So
chatter what you will. For such

puzzlement there is no pill. I'll say it
once and once again: t'is all but
guaranteed you'll ne'er find another
quite like me. And time is scarce,
you'll see.

Geppetto
And what would you have me do?

Piece of wood
Put your foot on the accelerator!
Bring on a new day, a new me! By
hammer, by saw, by late night
lantern hour after hour, as long as
your arts and crafts may last, and
strength of wrist and forearm. Until
you've lit a torch to the bark of my
being and released me for all time.

Medley of Marionettes
My, he is a fine one; did you get a
load of that diction? Those words?
Who the hell does he think he is,
anyway? Release him? Sure, and
while you're at it go down to the local
prison and release all the thieves

and assassins.

    Geppetto (to Piece of Wood)
You give me far too much credit. But
then, this is no wooden speech. How
does a lifeless fragment of the forest
come by such notions, words and
eloquence?

    Piece of Wood
For whatever else I may be, I am,
alas, Italian — every knot, sinew and
grandiloquence.

    Geppetto
Then what is your name? (looks to
the Marionettes) Did I just ask a
piece of wood its name?

    Tallest of Marionettes
Afraid so. First sign of
Woodsheimer's Disease. There's a
clinic two blocks away.

Smallest of Marionettes
What's worse? Bark beetle or
Woodsheimer's?

Piece of Wood
Pinocchio.

Geppetto (makes the sign of the
cross on his chest)
Mama Mia! Blasphemy! Pinocchio?
THE Pinocchio?

Pinocchio
What, there is another? Are you not
Geppetto, THE Geppetto?

Marionettes
This is mightily confusing. Are we
Marionettes or are we not? Is this the
world, or somewhere else?

Tiniest of the Marionettes
I knew something was wrong, the
minute we had that seven point six
this morning. All my screws are
loose.

Geppetto
My clever little would-that-he-could
— (looking at the Marionettes) — By
the way, that was a good one and
you flatheads didn't even get it!"
(Then to Pinocchio): My little man,
whatever your origins, let's see what
can be done about this strange
predicament. You realize, of course,
that you will confuse posterity by
calling yourself Pinocchio.

Pinocchio
What if I called myself Posterity?

Geppetto
Pinocchio is better.

Pinocchio
Pinocchio it is, then.

Geppetto
Of course, it's like naming yourself
Papageno and singing in German.
Or worse, Tamino, before
proclaiming,'An image of enchanted

loveliness, such as no eyes have
ever beheld.'

Pinocchio
You've hit upon it exactly. That's me!

Geppetto
No, that's Mozart.

Pinocchio
Don't know him. But I implore you,
there's no time to waste.

Marionettes
Did you hear that? Implore. A dumb
piece of wood *implores* Geppetto.
Such arrogance from a knot in the
woods pretending to be our national
hero. Good luck!

Geppetto (confused, looking at
Pinocchio, then to the Marionettes,
finally throwing up his hands)
Alright, why not! Stranger things
have happened.

Marionettes
Like when, for instance? (They
shake their heads, having lost the
battle, resigned to whatever destiny
may bring to their poor little place in
the world, which has now become
more crowded and more uncertain).

Geppetto sets to work, sawing away, staining the
wood dark, massaging it and revealing more and
more the unisexual young teenager we'll come to
know as Pinocchio.

Geppetto (halting for a moment)
But you must promise me one thing.

Pinocchio
Yes?

Geppetto
That once I have finished, you will be
good, true blue and kind. And not go
around thinking you really are
Pinocchio, when that would be
heresy, not to mention impossible
since he lived long ago.

Marionettes
He still lives. (Looking at one another
slightly confused, scratching their
heads) – doesn't he?

Pinocchio
But that's not one thing, that's four
things.

Geppetto
What? What are you talking about?

Pinocchio
You said promise one thing? But
then you said, 'Be Good,' that's one.
Be 'true blue,' that makes two; 'be
kind,' that's three; 'and not go around
thinking I'm who I am, Pinocchio,'
that's four.

Geppetto
And not be a smart-ass.

Pinocchio
That's five. My but we are
demanding.

Geppetto
A tree that can count!

Marionettes
Yeah, a regular lord of the rings.

Pinocchio
But I *am* a smart-ass!

Geppetto
Indeed you are. You must learn
respect for your elders like every
proper Italian.

Pinocchio
You underestimate the age of the
forest from whence I come.
Moreover, did you know that Italy is
the fifth most densely populated
country in Europe? Why it harbors
490 persons per square mile, and
the largest percentage of old people
with few leaves left, 25% by 2030. Of
course they are outnumbered by
trees. But still, no tree ever smoked
cigars, drank vermouth half the night,

got arthritis, or farted in the grocery
store.

>   Geppetto (leaning on his axe with an
>   incredulous fascination)
> I didn't know that. (Looks to the
> Marionettes) – Did you know that?
> (They all shrug ignorance)

>   Pinocchio
> Making her forests the oldest in the
> world, and me, the oldest smart-ass
> in the oldest forest, in the oldest
> country. So get busy!

>   Geppetto (amazed – to the
> audience)
> He read it!

>   Pinocchio
> On the Internet!

>   Geppetto (a rough chuckle – to the
>   audience)
> On the Internet!

Pinocchio
Most of the trees in this forest are
broad-band.

Geppetto
Damnit, stop squirming and mouthing
off ... you're confusing me! I shall
carve a leg wherein belongs a nose.
And a mouth instead of a smart-ass!

Pinocchio (settling down as
Geppetto goes to work)
Smart-ass, wise-ass, whatever
works.

Geppetto starts carving him gently.

Pinocchio
Oh, don't stop. That feels sooooo ...
good!

Geppetto (looking up, then gets to
work, seriously carving away,
hammering, using various
mathematical tools of his trade
from that array hanging on his wall.

He is a true craftsman.)

Then he pauses to wipe the sweat from his brow
with a handkerchief in his trousers.

> Pinocchio
> I said don't stop!

> Geppetto
> Shhh! Just one must more alteration
> to the fantastico-gyration. A nail there
> (hammers) and screw there (turns)
> and presto! A mirror please!

One of the Marionettes leaning against the wall of
the hut hands Geppetto a mirror saying, "Frankly, it
looks more like Frankenstein, if you ask me."

Geppetto hands the mirror to Pinocchio who takes
it in his right hand — which is slowly coming to life
— and admires this new handiwork of the creator.

> Pinocchio
> Those cheeks…those eyes. But what
> a surprise. Somewhere between a
> Rodin and a Little Abner. My old

friend Enrico Mazzanti would surely
approve.

Geppetto
Who?

Pinocchio
He was a fine artist who used to run
around painting all of the trees. I was
young but he tripped on one of my
branches and the rest is history.

Tallest of the Marionettes
I still think he looks like Frankenstein.

Geppetto (gazing upon his creation)
No, he is definitely Pinocchio,
because he reminds me of
Pinoochia, a woman I once loved.
Oh my. Even her memory still makes
me quake.

Pinocchio
Like an aspen. Aspen quake. I know
this for a fact. I had a neighbor, you
see. Whole glen of them. Prettiest

leaves for miles around.

Geppetto
Worse lad. Much worse. She was
Saintly as she was beautiful, with
powers that defied description. A
creature both wild and stately, and
full of surprises, the saddest of which
was her disappearance years ago
from the village. Some say she was
transformed by her goodness into a
spirit of the forest, where I searched
long years for her. That's how I
became a woodsmen. In fact, my
true calling was the choir. Handel.
Monteverdi ...

Marionettes (mocking)
Ahhh, a little choir boy forced by love
to become a rude crude woodsmen.

Geppetto (shaking his head; to
         Pinocchio)
Don't listen to them. They're just
wooden puppets, one more foolish
than the next.

Marionettes
Oh, and he isn't just an old piece of
pine, we suppose?

Geppetto
I don't know what to think. You
bumbling bastardly bunch of
brainless wine-guzzling boobs.

Marionettes (looking at one another)
Who is he talking about?
Geppetto
But you need just one final touch,
don't move, be very very still. (He
applies one last little tweak). Finito!
You're on your own, lad!

Pinocchio (taking a deep breath,
catching the first scent of his
freedom, slowly stands, turns, twists
and then without warning, leaps
forward)
I taste the first joy of my legs, and the
rush of my senses seeking out the
horizon.

Medley of Marionettes
A child on his first adventure is a
dangerous business. He didn't even
say thank you. Caution, Pinocchio,
for all is not as it seems in this world.
We know!

Pinocchio
And caution to you, too, with your
puppets for brains. For hear me well:
I have a mind of pine and hands that
shine. And legs which feel no want of
energy. All coated in linseed. But
wait, what's that? (he comes to a
sudden halt before the window).

Geppetto
The great outdoors, my dear
Pinocchio. Where it is cold and about
to snow. Remember? But now you
are more than a tree, and lacking
bark and branches to keep you
warm. You are a freak, a hybrid,
without a battery charger.

But suddenly Pinocchio is out the door in a flash.

Geppetto lunges after him only to see the young creature racing away at a frightful speed into the village.

> Medley of Marionettes
> That's one less to feed.

> Geppetto
> Come back!

> Marionettes
> Better to put the rascal out of your
> mind. For he's a troublemaker,
> probably already joined a gang,
> hanging out at the disco, and soon
> he'll be dealing in drugs. Next move,
> to Sicily. You watch!

Geppetto hunkers down in a chair and laments his loss.

> Marionettes (among themselves)
> Poor Geppetto.

> Geppetto
> My one chance at happiness. A real

son, or was he simply a monster of
ungratefulness?

Medley of debating Marionettes
I'll wager on the monster theory.

Taller Marionette
He'd bring ruin to this household.
Hunchback Marionette
Or glory. Think, my friends, hard as
that might be for some of you: who
among us ever had the courage to
run out that door?

Fourth Marionette
True. Many a days I thought of it, but
lacked the strength.

Tiniest Marionette
Dexterity.

Geppetto
Stupidity!

Marionettes in Unison
Let's face it, we all lacked the

inspiration!

>   Tallest of the Marionettes
> No point rubbing it in, so good
> riddance, I say. (Spits on the floor
> and rubs it in)

Off-stage we hear a tumult of voices and the crashing of carriages, and the rearing of frightened horses. A loud commotion comes nearer, then accusations are hurled at Geppetto, who listens with fear to all this from inside his hut.

Suddenly, the crowd arrives with a policeman at his door, holding an out-of-breath Pinocchio by the hand.

>   Poliziotto
> Geppetto, old friend, this time you've
> outdone yourself. Surely you know
> that human cloning is illegal? The Ad
> Hoc Committee on the International
> Convention Against Reproduction
> Technology In-Vitro et cetera et
> cetera.

Geppetto

But that's preposterous. See for
yourself, he is merely a stick of wood
with some fancywork thrown in.
(Geppetto starts towards Pinocchio
with a wrench and screwdriver to
prove his point, but the policeman
holds him back)

Poliziotto

You go too far, old man, for that is
human flesh, I saw him shat on the
sidewalk, a Class Two Misdemeanor.

Geppetto

You what!

Poliziotto

This boy has feelings, and more than
mere wood pulp in his belly. Say
something. (knocks Pinocchio on the
head)

Pinocchio

Alas, the spark of poetry excites my
veins. I am the spitting image of a

mother who exists only in my
dreams. And yet, to find her, I would
take great pains.

Poliziotto
You see! Poignant confession of his
humanity.

Geppetto
I swear I found him in the forest, near
a burnt-out fire, among a stack of
logs, no use to any man. I turned him
into something, that is true. The
latest in sophisticated puppetry,
nothing more.

Poliziotto
This is out of my hands. A question
of ultimate discretion, of
deoxyribonucleic acid, and about
which no civilized society can afford
to be placid.

Geppetto
Absurd!

Marionettes (perplexed among
themselves)
Deoxy? Ribo?

Poliziotto
A matter for the authorities. You'll
come with me.The policeman ushers
Geppetto away towards the village.

Medley of Marionettes
We'll just scratch together some bail
money and that will be the end of it.
And better for all of us!

Night descends on the village. Stars seen in the
backdrop, scattered through a lightly falling snow.
All the Marionettes are snoring soundly.

Pinocchio enters the darkened room, shakes the
snow out of his hair, and collapses in a chair after
who knows what adventures.

Pinocchio
My goodness that was fun! To jump
out of trees on unsuspecting postal
workers, steal dirty magazines from

the stores, and lamb shanks from the
paws of obese geezers. Clearly mine
is not the fate of other boys. I am my
own man now.

> Voice of a Cricket
> We'll see about that!

The Marionettes are awakened by all the noise.
They light the central oil lamp.

> Pinocchio (peering into the diffused
> half-light)
> Who is that?

A giant cricket — the size of a small child dressed
effectively as a cricket — moves forward out of the
shadows.

> Cricket
> Pardon my saying so, young man,
> but you have neither the dignity of a
> puppet, nor common sense of an
> average insect. In fact, you strike the
> same pose as that abominable
> fellow, Mussolini, famed for his

hatred not only of crickets, but
everybody.

Pinocchio
What? How dare you! A bug, no less;
impious, measly, scum of creation, I
have a mind to stamp you out.

Cricket (fearless)
Listen to me, fool; others pull the
strings. You have one chance to
escape the history that has already
been pre-ordained for you.

Pinocchio
What are you talking about?

Cricket
To dispense henceforth with your
arrogant shenanigans and become a
source of pride to your maker. Go to
school and achieve high marks, and
make something of yourself, as your
father, Geppetto would want for you.
And most of all, be kind to all living
things, especially crickets like me.

A Marionette Mumbles
Stamp the bugger out. He's always
making noise.

Pinocchio
That's all?

Cricket
More than enough.

Pinocchio
Be kind to insects? Why I can do
that. On condition you get me
something to eat, for I am starving.
And some wood to burn, for I am
freezing.

Cricket
There's no food. Anyway, what was
that about lamb-shanks?

Pinocchio
I was just bragging. I don't even
know what they are.

Cricket
Geppetto is poor. And the same
goes for firewood.

Pinocchio
No food? No warmth? Then that
simply proves your theory of
goodness to be bankrupt. I'll have
none of it. Now scram before I really
do squash you to smithereens.

Pinocchio (searching frantically now
for a morsel to eat, making a ruckus)
There's got to be some food
somewhere!

Outside the storm intensifies, snow flurries
threatening to blow down the door, and bits of
snow getting through into the hut.

Pinocchio (shivering)
Now I'm really cold, too. And not so
much as a crumb of bread to satisfy
this hunger.

Medley of Marionettes
Mussolini calling for his fettuccini.
Pretty damned pathetic.

Pinocchio
Why, it's terrible to be a boy. Not-
withstanding lamb shanks and nasty
pranks. Perhaps if I had listened to
the cricket?

Cricket (hiding in a corner beside the
Marionettes)
You see! Perhaps there is still hope
for him after all.

Pinocchio
Of course, I could route the cricket
from his cranny, and eat him for my
dinner, thus avoid getting any
thinner. That might be simpler than a
total reformation of my confirmation.

Medley of Marionettes (to the cricket)
Hope, is it? Fat chance. To that little
creep, you're just a sack of protein.

>   Pinocchio
> I don't know what to do. If only
> Geppetto would come home, forgive
> my legs and natural curiosity, then I
> would surely turn a new corner,
> enroll at Rome in gynecology, or
> better yet serve tables at that
> Pizzaria down the street.

Suddenly, the Marionettes hear the arrival of
Geppetto and resume their frozen silence.

Geppetto enters his hut, brushes snow off his coat,
places a sack of food on the table, and a bundle of
firewood in the pit.

>   Geppetto
> There you are. What a mess of
> things. I had to convince the Collodi
> committee on ethics that your DNA
> was useless; and persuade those
> sitting on the Genoa assembly of
> Italian sovereignty that you were of
> no consequence whatsoever to the
> stability of the country, her market
> forces, fashion industry, or literary

tradition. That you were neither
Communist nor radical and would
promise not to deface sidewalks ever
again.

Pinocchio
But, if I might be so bold – useless?
Of no consequence?

Geppetto
Well, perhaps a slight overstatement.

Pinocchio
Then who, what am I?

Geppetto (finally conceding —)
I believe the evidence will show you
are my rightful son.

Pinocchio (overcome with emotions,
    embracing his father)
Father, thank you, thank you. I will be
good. I promise. Now may we eat,
get warm, and talk of old times?

Medley of Marionettes
He's bound to regret it!

Geppetto lights the fire, and serves Pinocchio a
long submarine sandwich.

Geppetto
It's called a submarine sandwich,
large. Extra avocado and jalapeno
peppers. You're not allergic to
peppers, are you?

Pinocchio
Love peppers! Lived near a pepper
tree, once. She died in the warm
snap of '07.

Geppetto
You mean cold snap?

Pinocchio
Are you kidding? It was the warmest
storm on record. Everyone in the
forest was wishing they had air
conditioners!

Geppetto
I remember it as being quite cold.

Pinocchio
Cold? It was a heat spell, the worst
on record. Ask the beetles, the mites,
the spiders, not to mention the
leaves. They'll tell you the real deal,
here. You have no idea what a few
degrees one way or the other mean
to a Helluode whose trusted to
equanimity for millions of years. They
don't take well to change.

Geppetto
What's a Helluode?

Pinocchio
They eat the termites, but so slowly
the termites hardly know they're
being devoured. More like a slow-
acting palliative, a morphine drip. Of
course, you'd have to be a tree to
know about such things. We provide
all the shade for the fungi and termite
mounds. And it's just as bad for most

of the trees and birds and squirrels.
Not to mention raccoons, truffles,
and bats. We managed to save the
masked owls and crimson tanagers
that were occupying their branches
but we could do nothing for the
Helluodes, the snails and the slugs.
Not to mention the poor wild horses
attracted to the odd persimmon lying
around. Makes them do cartwheels,
which is never recommended for a
Mustang.

Geppetto
Very interesting. It may have felt
warm to you, but it's damn cold for
the likes of me. Especially on a day
like this.

Marionettes
A regular Mother Teresa. All this
scientific mumbo jumbo. What about
us? This piece of wood is posing as
a biologist. When all it's really doing
is deliberately confusing the subject:
food!

Geppetto
Yeah yeah ... (tosses them several
submarine-like sandwiches)

Act 1
Scene 2

A snowy landscape. The sun is shining on the
village as Pinocchio -dressed in his father's coat,
carrying a schoolbook, heads towards school
singing.

> Pinocchio
> Aren't I the luckiest piece of wood in
> the whole world? Geppetto's very
> own coat right off his back, what a
> great heart; and food in my belly.
> Without his love this brat of bramble
> wood a mannequin would have
> remained, low-brow, unlettered, not
> one pinch of tenderness. But now, I
> shall soon be memorizing Petrarch
> and doing advanced mathematics.

Suddenly, Pinocchio arrives before a small crowd
gathered before a puppet theater. The impresario
– fire-eater, a famed femme fatale – is on hand to
welcome the paying guests and commence the
show, while her ticket master works the crowd
taking money for admission.

Pinocchio
Hey dude, Che passa?

Ticket Master (Bruno)
Magic puppets. Pay your hundred
Lira or move on.

Pinocchio
My, how I would like to see that. But I
am hastening to the Roman Senate,
and then shall check in at the finest
university. Anyway, I never carry
cash.

Ticket Master (sizing up his bright
red coat made of the finest wool and
fancy boots)
The finest university, is it? And isn't
that strange, I'd swear I heard the
Senate had adjourned for the
holidays, and all the Professors are
at the conference in Cophenhagen.

Pinocchio
A holiday? Which holiday?
Conference? Where's Cophen-

hagen?

Ticket Master
Why it's puppet day, surely you've
heard? The first performance
minutes away.

Pinocchio (thinking over the news)
I suppose I could stay for just one
show ...

Ticket Master
Not if you don't have a thousand Lira.

The puppets now march onto the little stage.
Pinocchio knows each and every one of the
Marionettes, who have tormented him from the
beginning.

Pinocchio (annoyed)
Wait a minute: Those buggers? You
pay THEM to perform? Little pricks,
big pricks, poopheads, gutter trash,
I'm telling you.

Ticket Master

Ahh. You must be the famous
Pinocchio. Tell you what, I'll swap
you an entrance ticket for that
mangy, worthless outdated coat of
yours. (Ticket master checks the
inside top collar) You see, these
days, without a label that reads
`Made in Milan' it's worthless. Go on
then, give me the coat and you can
see your friends make jerks of
themselves. In fact, you can join
them on stage and I'll even introduce
you to Mademoiselle Fire-Eater.

Pinocchio (thinking it over)

It's my father's coat. He gave it to me
on my birthday. He said it was my
13th, meaning I am now a teenager.

Ticket Master

Take it or leave it. Anyway, he would
be proud of your business savvy as
you prepare for your college years.
College is not cheap, my lad. Tuition
has gone through the roof.

Pinocchio
Still, it was a gift. He is a poor man,
you know.

Ticket Master
Done business for years with your
old man. Hard worker, he is. Harder
than most. They don't make 'um like
that anymore. Real labor, hard day's
work. Nothing to show for it. And
fallen on hard times, he has. Didn't
know he had a kid? Tell you what,
just to help you out, a ticket and two
gold coin coins for that coat. You can
be sure Geppetto will be grateful for
some share of your newfound
fortune.

Pinocchio (making sense of if all)
Exactly! Make that four gold pieces
and I'll give up my new schoolbook
as well. That's even better savvy.

Ticket Master
I said two gold pieces.

Pinocchio
Four or the deal's off.

Ticket Master
Tell you what, throw in those fancy
leather boots of yours and that
coloring book and you have a deal.

Pinocchio (gleefully)
You strike a hard bargain. Who
needs boots. And I've already read
the book.

Ticket Master
Shows about to begin. You better
hurry to get your seat.

Pinocchio takes the four gold coins into his pocket,
then hands over his boots, schoolbook and coat to
the ticket master and enters the circus-like tent.
The Marionettes all see him and rejoice with high
hopes. Pinocchio is greeted by the hunch backed
Mademoiselle Fire-Eater who helps him up onto

the stage, past the onlookers.

> Fire-Eater
> And you are?

> Pinocchio
> Pinocchio, son of Geppetto.

> Fire-Eater (looking him over)
> Have we a place for another puppet?

> Harlequin (one of the Marionettes)
> I will vouch for him but only if he
> gives me ones of his gold pieces.

> Pinocchio
> Forget it.

> Punchinello (another Marionette)
> He'll never fit in. The most stubborn
> stump of wood I've ever met.

> Pinocchio
> I am no stump. More like a runt.

Ms. Rose (a third Marionette)
I doubt he's a puppet at all, with
those crazy bone and big ears on the
lookout for the slightest opportunity.
Look at his dimple, finger nails,
sweetly-crisscrossed eyelashes, as if
he were some movie star. But there's
something mightily astray that starts
behind his eyes. And comes from the
core of his errant brain. No, definitely
not one of us. And please,
Pinocchio? Like we're some
collective dim-wit? You were
published in 1883. This is the 21st
century. Who does he think he is?
He's a fraud. A danger to society.

Voices from the Theatergoers
And the one that caused the
commotion. Raced through the
streets. Shat on the sidewalk. Broke
through a pane glass window to get
at a chocolate doughnut. And
brought the cops down on poor old
Geppetto.

Fire-Eater
Pinocchio, eh? Geppetto told me all
about it. Shouldn't you be off to the
academy today?

Pinocchio
But it is a holiday, Ma'am. Haven't
you heard?

Fire-Eater
What I've heard is that your father
paid for a year's education at the
finest Prep-school in all of Tuscany
cash up-front. Sold all his
Marionettes to get you admitted. And
this is how you re-pay his kindness?
Bruno, give him back his coat, his
boots, his schoolbook.

Ticket Master
But boss, I paid him four gold
doppiettas.

Fire-Eater
Your loss, Bruno. You never did
have much of a business sense. I

would have fired you long ago if it weren't for the fact I made the mistake of marrying your father. If it had been me, I would have paid the kid a half-sovrano and — maybe — a quarter doppie. Anyway, let him keep the gold coins. He'll need them. And we've had a good season. (To Pinocchio) Now take some advice young man, from a woman whose been around: there's nothing like a good education and loving parents to give you an edge on a brutal world.

Medley of Marionettes
Nine lives, this one has. He's a lucky boy. But I'll take a brutal world any day over homework.

Pinocchio
Work? What's that?

Fire-Eater
Don't listen to them. That's why they'll be making minimum wage for their whole miserable existence.

Because they frown upon homework.
The Marionettes all start to perform
for the crowd which has assembled
before them inside the colorful tent.

Dancing, singing, making merriment. Pinocchio
watches this winter reverie with some confusion,
wanting to join in, but feeling alien.

      Pinocchio
I can't explain the sensation. I'm one
of them, but I'm not. I want to dance,
but I also feel the urgings of the
forest. Of leaves flying through the
air, of being part of all that and the
owls, tanagers even the Great Blue
Herons – heavy birds to be sure –
nesting in my family tree. Who am I?
Where have I come from? Where am
I going? To school? Towards what
end. Home? Or far away?
And what the hell is this business
about `work' – I don't like the sound
of it.

Fire-Eater
I'll tell you where: to school by day,
your father's hut by night. Some day
you'll meet a beautiful girl. Fall in
love. Unless you fall pray to any
more distractions, in which case it
could go very badly for you, and for
Geppetto – as well. Do you
understand?

Pinocchio
Loud and clear. Good-bye, then. I
promise to be a fine fellow, free of
temptation. No more horsing around
for me.

Fire-Eater (pats Pinocchio on the
     head)
Good boy! (Then she smacks Ticket
Master on the head) Even a piece of
wood outsmarts my own idiot for a
son!

Ticket Master (whining)
Little creep, took my gold!
The Marionettes (all sing their

farewells).
Dexterity.
Stupidity!
Let's face it, we all lacked his
inspiration!
Good riddance, I say. What does he
know that we don't know, eh?

Act 2
Scene 1

Daytime. A storm is brewing. Pinocchio has come to a bewildering juncture in the countryside. A sign points in half-dozen different directions. One way says Rome, another the Fields of Golden Miracles. It is 384,403 kilometers to the Moon, 99 kilometers to Venice, and 14 kilometers to the Inn of the Red Crawdad. While school is indicated as being 10 kilometers to the north. A farmer is walking by and stops to warn him.

> Farmer
> Good day, my fine fellow.

> Pinocchio
> Good day to you as well.

> Farmer
> By your look of nuttiness I would wager that you are not from these parts?

> Pinocchio
> I'm on my way to the Roman Senate

but have to stop in at school. Have
you seen one, by chance?

Farmer
Better to seek your fortune out
among the fields.

Pinocchio
Doing what?

Farmer
Working, of course! These are hard
times — terrorists at large, oil spills
and mad cow, and no amount of
schooling will prepare you for that!

Pinocchio
Mad cow? Work? The real world?
Surely you are over-reacting.

Farmer
Son, dangers abound. On this road
especially, as it leads to Rome. As
for school, if you insist, there's one
about ten kilometers up the road. But
you're wasting your time. None of us

went to school. Wouldn't you prefer a
job picking grapes, enjoying all those
late night hay-rides?

Pinocchio
I'm allergic to hay. And work is
positively against my religion. And as
for dangers, I assure you I can take
care of myself. I have a hard head.

Farmer
Well good luck to you, then.

The farmer continues on his way while Pinocchio
studies the sign, suddenly struck with fear by what
the farmer said.

Pinocchio
Oh dear, did I speak a tad too
hastily? What if he was right? On one
hand, these adults are a sack of
contradictions. On the other hand a
certain troubling wisdom prevails ....
no. I promised Fire-Eater. And owe
my life to Geppetto. School and a life
of merit for Pinocchio. Nothing,

absolutely nothing shall dissuade
me.

Pinocchio now sees two well-dressed men – not
unlike the traditional Mazzanty-drawings – as in
bipedal Musketeers — approaching. They are
speaking to one another.

> Fox
> Look yonder? Could that be the
> famed Pinocchio we've heard so
> much about?

> Cat
> Why, by his noble bearing and
> magnificent countenance I believe
> you've hit it on the nose.

> Pinocchio
> Who is that?

> Fox
> Monsieurs Foxworth

> Cat
> And Catwell

Fox
At your service, Signore.

Pinocchio pauses. Not sure he trusts these two.

Catwell
You appear befuddled beneath the
signpost for Central Italy. One way,
big city life, with all its do's and
don't's. To the South, Easter Island,
but there are no bunnies there, from
what I've heard. And to the Far East,
well, only the bare margins of
existence.

Foxworth
And to the North – may the very word
disappear from the Italian language
– scuola. Or escola in Portuguese.
Shkola in Russian.

Catwell
École, in my native tongue, French.

Pinocchio
But you know so many languages.

Surely you learned them all in
school?

Foxworth
Nope, we learned them in the West,
where the sun forever sets, you no
doubt have noticed mention of the
fields of golden miracles.

Pinocchio
I did. What's that?

Catwell (looking at Fox)
What's that, he asks.

Foxworth
A prudent query, to be sure. Even if
he is a mere piece of wood.

Pinocchio
In that you are mistaken.

Catwell
Well, there is one way to prove it.

Pinocchio
Tell me, then.

Foxworth
Very simple, and profitable, to boot.

Pinocchio
Yes? As you can see I have no
boots. I gave them up for four pieces
of gold. (He shows them the gold)

Foxworth
Well then, you are in luck. (Looking
at Cat) Should I reveal to him?

Catwell
Why not.

Pinocchio
Oh please! You must!

Catwell
Then you must.

Foxworth
Right. But you must keep it a secret.

Very very few Italians know about
this. Why, if the secret were to get
out, there would be a rush on all the
banks. The stock market would
collapse.

Catwell
The Lira, or Euro if you prefer,
devalued to nothing.

Foxworth
Pension funds, not to mention every
pensione, ruined. Food lines would
multiply, fighting would break out,
mobs would attack bowling alleys to
get at the French fries.

Catwell
There'd be a run on Snickers Bars.

Foxworth
Not to mention bottles of Pellegrino
Water.

Pinocchio
My goodness, what a terrible picture

you paint. What can I do?

      Catwell (to Foxworth)
Yeah, why not. I think he can be
trusted to keep a secret, don't you?

      Foxworth (looking Pinocchio up and
      down)
Hmm…. Not sure.

      Pinocchio
Yes I can. Absolutely. I am steadfast.
You can trust me.

      Foxworth
Well then, listen carefully. You must
plant one gold coin tonight, pee on it
for moisture, and tomorrow a
thousand will grow up in its place.
Inflation minus depreciation equals
the sum of imagination without even
a hint of economic stagnation. That is
where every clever Italian has made
his riches.

Catwell

And subsequently acquired villas,
linguini factories, and a seat on the
stock exchange.

Foxworth

A few have become television
moguls, like our current Prime
Minister. Although there are risks.
Broken noses, that sort of thing.

Pinocchio

Broken noses? Well, as you can see
I have a tiny nose, and because it is
made of wood, it would be very
difficult to break.

Foxworth

May I?

He reaches forward to touch Pinocchio's nose.

Foxworth

You are quite right. It is wooden. You
have nothing to worry about, in that
case.

Pinocchio
So that's the secret to riches!

Catwell
Yes, but remember what we told you.
Not a word of this to anyone. It was
just by pure chance we should all
meet up like this beneath the very
center of Italy. Otherwise, if not for
this miraculous coincidence of timing,
we should have kept the secret to
ourselves.

Foxworth
But we are feeling very generous
today, aren't we Cat. (Foxworth kicks
Catwell)

Catwell (coughing)
Oh, indeed. Generous to a fault. Of
course, you are a mere child. You
can't be expected to have investment
capital.

Foxworth
The tragedy of the young.

Catwell
Yes, always the case. Youth is
wasted on the old and decrepit.

Foxworth
To miss out on the bull market of the
century for want of a few gold coins.

Pinocchio (reaching in his coat)
But I do! I have four pieces of gold.

Catwell
What? You must be joking? Let me
see?

Pinocchio holds them forth.

Catwell
Well what do you know! That makes
you the next Caesar.

Foxworth
Or Pope by the time he's finished
peeing! You'll need to drink a lot of
vino, however.

> Catwell
>
> To build up the urine content. You
> see, we cats know all about the art of
> peeing.

> Pinocchio
>
> Just not on the sidewalk, right?

Catwell and Foxworth look at one another, slightly uncertain, then –

> Foxworth
>
> Right. In the field, where you must
> bury those sovereigns.

> Catwell
>
> After tomorrow, you'll be in the top
> zero-point-one percent of Italy's
> superstars. The billionaire's club.
> Congratulations!

> Pinocchio
>
> Oh, my goodness! How might I ever
> thank you?

Foxworth
No need. Banish the thought. This is
Christmas week, is it not? And we
are feeling very generous indeed.

Catwell
But we must also instruct him on how
to elude paying taxes.

Pinocchio
What's that?

Catwell
You don't want to know.

Foxworth
Anyway, they can't tax a piece of
wood, right?

Catwell
Well, they could. They tax forest
managers, woodcutters, villagers in
the forest…. hmmm.

But while the Catwell and Foxworth are discussing
the in's and out's of Italian taxation theory,

Pinocchio is suddenly getting very nervous,
remembering what he was supposed to do.

Pinocchio
Gentleman, I'm a little worried.

Catwell
Worried? About becoming a
billionaire?

Pinocchio
Oh no, that sound's wonderful. It's
just that I made a few promises, you
see. I am supposed to go to school.

Both the Foxworth and Catwell burst out laughing.

Foxworth
Prison more like it!

Catwell
Filled with losers. When riches await
you just around the corner.

Foxworth
Do you know how many fools did it

the hard way — spent years in
school … and for what?
So that they could perpetuate the
misery of their parents and end up
working for the government in some
dreary eight-to-six, earning twenty-
thousand a year and breathing in
fumes as you fight your way home in
commuter traffic and a vehicle that
get's flat tires, the gear shift goes
bad, transmission costs a fortune to
replace, and all for what?

    Pinocchio
Eight-to-six? Doesn't that involve
menial labor?

    Foxworth (groans just how much
menial labor it really portends)

    Catwell
And having screaming children who
need their diapers changed
continuously.

Foxworth
College tuitions.

Catwell
Prostate cancer.

Foxworth
The price of a new suit, razor blade,
shaving cream, polished shoes.
Italian clothes do not come cheap.

Catwell
Mafioso lurking round every corner,
tapping the till.

Foxworth
Mother-in-laws always laying guilt
trips on you.

Catwell
Having to fly on holidays with all your
kids, lines a block long at security.

Foxworth
Early death.

Pinocchio

None of that is me, truly.

Foxworth

I didn't think he seemed the type.

Catwell

Maybe not. But there's only one way
to find out.

Pinocchio

So all I do is plant the coins and pee
on them?

Catwell

Exactly. Can you believe it! The most
elegant solution, yet it takes a genius
to figure it out.

Foxworth

Like the lightbulb. Edison was Italian.

Pinocchio

He was?

Catwell
As was Henry Ford not to mention
Cat Stevens.

Pinocchio
You're kidding?

Foxworth
Nope, so too the Marx Brothers,
Bach, Beethoven, Buddha, Gandhi,
Obama –

Pinocchio
Obama? I thought he was from
Africa?

Foxworth
Please. Anybody that smart has to
be Italian to the core. Not to mention
Al Capone, Abraham Lincoln, Bugsy
Siegel, George Washington, Charlie
Chaplin. All good Italians who loved
their mothers and went to Church.

Pinocchio
I knew that. And to think, if I hadn't

met you two noblemen. What a
dreary life was in store for me.
Prostate cancer! I don't even know
what it is or want to know. Do trees
have prostates? Well then, to heck
with school. I will be contemporary.

Catwell
Avant garde.

Foxworth
A venture capitalist. Soon you'll be
driving a Bugatti Veyron, or
Lamborghini Reventon, 3-point-three
seconds to hit sixty miles an hour, or
Maserati Quattroporte S – that's the
one all the supermodels prefer. You'll
be living the dream.

Pinocchio
Just think what Geppetto will say
when I return to him with thousands
of gold coins instead of four. And
driving a Quattroporte S!. Wow! How
can I ever thank you both?

Foxworth
A hero for our time. Like Lermontov.
Also Italian.

Catwell
But we must go on ahead and let
them know.

Foxworth
Let them know?

This time Catwell kicks Foxworth, as if under the
table.

Catwell
You know? The supermodels. To let
them know in advance.

Foxworth
Ahh. Right. Of course. To let them
know.

Pinocchio
Let them know?

Catwell
Very important, listen well: That you'll
be coming at midnight. So they can
prepare the ground. Roll out the red
carpet. We will meet you there. Just
continue straight in that direction.
One hour, that's all it takes.

Pinocchio
Got it. One hour. Red carpet.
Midnight. Supermodels. Prepare the
ground.

Foxworth and Catwell bow most courteously and
make their departure.

The Sun has set. A Moon rises above snowy
barren fields. A cold wind.

Pinocchio (walking restlessly in the
directly of the miracle fields, sings
with great joy, pride and
expectations)
If only my mother and father were
here to celebrate my good fortune.
What supreme happiness!

I am feeling faint-headed with glee.
Glee ... what a word ... allégresse, I
heard a snail call it, after eating a
primrose years ago one Spring
morning, as he crawled away,
leaving a trail of pure silver.

The stars rush into my veins and the
memory of hard times flows out to
sea. I am weightless.

The whole world teems with blithe
spirits now, urging me on towards
that tree canopy of desires and
hopes which – previously – had been
no more than a dull ache, registering
as an infinite pain low down in my
gut, where there was not the slightest
chance of bursting free, or declaring
my soul. Mon âme vraie. That much I
remember from all the gossip from
branch to branch.

Now, as the midnight hour
approaches, I see the world clearly.

What's more, I am feeling especially
compassionate. Once this business
is complete, I shall certainly
apologize to that cricket — buy him
his own little bungalow, and enshrine
a national monument to crickets.
Where would we all be without them,
their sweetly lulling arias, addulced
and sugared night.

As for Geppetto, I shall offer a
reward of a thousand, a million, ten
million doppias of solid gold for
whoever can find his Pinocchia. So
that they may live happily ever after.
And when they are reunited, I shall
throw the grandest party in all of
Italy.

Then buy them a castle in which to
live in happily ever after.

No more poverty.

No more uncertainty. Libyan

hamsines. German Foens. Egyptian
simooms.

I shall set aside a kingdom strictly for
Marionettes, and dignify those
puppets once and for all, even if they
are a gaggle of obnoxious little
goons.

And repay Fire-Eater a thousand
fold.

Everyone shall be rich. There will be
no work. No laws. No taxes. No
Roman Senate or stealth aircraft.
Just enough carbon dioxide, not too
much. Air conditioning and all the
pollination any country, or nation,
could desire.

A paradise. A paradise. A paradise.

Now we notice hiding behind bushes Foxworth and
Catwell ready to make their heinous moves.

Catwell
What's stealth aircraft?

Foxworth
You're asking me? You're the one
who says he enrolled in the
Sorbonne.

Catwell
Actually, it was cat obedience
school, in Lyon. Totally humiliating. I
had to learn the name of every kitty
litter in Europe, in both French and
Italian. Lettiera del gattino, OK, that's
sensible. But Civière de minou?
Please. How can any self-respecting
cat remember such nonsense?

Foxworth
That's nothing. I had to learn foxtrot
in German.

Catwell
What is it?

Foxworth
Foxtrot.

Catwell
You mock me.

Foxworth
It's true!

Catwell
What's more, French zookeepers
took the town's name literally. Lyon,
that is. They actually brought their
lions to class. How's that for unfair
competition. Their heads are five
times the size of mine. And oh my
god, their urine – it stinks!

Pinocchio hears something.

Pinocchio
But what? Who goes there?

Suddenly all hell breaks loose: he is attacked by
two rogues, dressed as bandits. We recognize
them as Foxworth and Catwell, but Pinocchio does

not.

>   Foxworth (drawing a dagger towards
> Pinocchio's neck) Your gold or your
> life, be quick about it, time is fleeting.

>   Pinocchio
> You can't hurt me for I have a
> wooden head, and jaws of steel.

He quickly reaches into his coat pocket and places
his four gold coins in his mouth.

>   Foxworth
> Is that so? And I suppose the blood
> that flows through this fleshy neck is
> also wooden?

A fight ensues, Pinocchio scratching, banging,
badgering and kicking with all his gusto. Foxworth
and Catwell charge, retrench, circle, ensnare and
beat him senseless trying to pry open his mouth to
get at the gold.
While Catwell holds the exhausted Pinocchio
down, Foxworth removes a rope and ties
Pinocchio upside down against a tree.

Foxworth

That should make you feel right at
home. By the time we return in the
morning, all that silly blood rushing
upside down shall have rendered
you even more stupid than you
already are. That's when we will
seize our prize, and we may just slice
off your head for sport.

Catwell

Or for firewood at our celebration
barbecue tomorrow night!

Foxworth

And by the way, you're the invited
guest! Ha-ha-ha.

Foxworth and Catwell leave Pinocchio to suffer.

Act 2
Scene 2

Dawn rising. Pinocchio hangs upside down crying, exhausted, no longer capable of struggling. As the light increases he sees that there is an enchanted cottage not all that far from the tree to which he's tied. And three Angels in the guise of human-sized peregrine falcons coming towards him, gently-fanning their wings.

> Pinocchio
Falcons. I recognize you. Gyre
Falcons, in migration from
Greenland, right? How about helping
me out, please!

> First Falcon (kneeling down to
> examine the poor Pinocchio)
Cut the rope!

The Second Falcon swings her talon and easily cuts the rope, thus freeing Pinocchio, who immediately takes his gold from his mouth and replaces it into his pocket. While the Third Falcon flutters her wings to keep him cool.

Pinocchio
Whoever you are, thank you. But
there's little time to waste. The
rogues who did this to me are bound
to come back any minute.

Pinocchio tries to stand but falls back down. He is
weak, bruised and wounded.

First Falcon
You're hurt. But don't worry. You've
got higher powers looking over you,
now. They shall determine whether
you are deserving, or not.

Pinocchio
Deserving? But my family provided
nesting materials for falcons for
generation after generation —

Second Falcon
Shhh! We know all about you.

Pinocchio
Say, how are your cousins doing in
India?

      Third Falcon
Long Billed Griffons?

      Pinocchio
That's the one.

      Third Falcon
Major bummer. DDT. Going extinct.

      Pinocchio
I'm so sorry. The way I feel right now,
I am too.

Together, the three large falcons help Pinocchio
into the inner courtyard of the enchanted cottage
and lay him down on a downy chaise longue with
silk-embroidered pillows.

A human sized Mr. Crow and Pinocchio's former
acquaintance, the Giant Cricket, are standing by.

      Mr. Crow (stepping up to his chaise
      longue)
I cannot say whether he is living or
dying. But there is an aura about him
that would suggest he's on his last

breath. Next stop, a grave.

Pinocchio
No. I must protest. I am beaten, but
very much alive!

Mr.Crow
We will see. I've lived half my life
beside the freeway between Rome
and Milan and know very well the
difference between a live one and a
dead one, not that it matters. I mean,
if I'm really hungry, no offense.

Giant Cricket
I know this good-for-nothing. If he is
alive, better for the world that he
should be dead.

Pinocchio
Cricket! But I was just singing your
praises last night!

Cricket
To whom, the frozen fields of dead
risotto?

Pinocchio
I thought it was corn.

Cricket
Dead risotto.

Pinocchio
Lovely. And you utter the words with such, such melancholy. A true poet. Well, anyway, I'd made elaborate plans to buy you your own private bungalow, for what it's worth. Even contracted the architect.

Cricket
His name?

Pinocchio
How can you expect me to remember his name at a time like this?

Cricket
Where are the plans? Let me see them.

Pinocchio
They're not written down, they're in
the architect's head.

Cricket
Right.

Pinocchio
But it's true. Frank Gehry, that's it.
The one who worked magic with that
Disney Hall in the New World. My
goodness thanks to him, Bilbaos
abound, Bilbo in Basque, filled with
artsyfartsies ... Anyway, you can
surely see by now, I'm different. A
man of taste, learning, wide
experience.

Cricket
Different, alright. Definitely dead. The
Blue Fairy need not even bother
meeting him.

Pinocchio (singing to the Three
Falcon Angels, Mr. Crow and
Cricket)The Blue Fairy? Wait. The

Blue Fairy?

> First Falcon
> Well, that's a bit harsh, Cricket. I say
> he deserves another chance.

> Second Falcon
> I suppose so.

> Third falcon
> You're both too soft. But that makes
> three of us. We are Angels, after all.

> Cricket
> Fine. Of course, if it were me, I'd
> leave him tied to the tree where he
> belongs. Actually, anybody who even
> jokes about harming insects belongs
> beside Il Duce, buried in Predappio,
> but what do I care. I have my
> pension, and he's just a bad
> memory.

All three Angels sing a beguiling vibrato, fluttering
their wings, and eliciting from inside the cottage
the Blue Fairy, who emerges swathed in an

otherworldly azure aureole.

The Blue Fairy kneels beside Pinocchio and
examines him.

>   Pinocchio (weakly, then turning over
>   in pain)
>   I feel as if I know you!

The Blue Fairy turns away in astonishment. She,
too, recognizes a familiar face.

>   Blue Fairy
>   What do I see? The face of time that
>   once took me away,
>   Carried me on a wind of desire into
>   the forest where I was lost,
>   Lost forever it seems.
>   Far from my home, parents, friends,
>   even the love of a man.
>   And into the strange alluring never
>   never world of spirits,
>   Where wood is not wood, and every
>   knot in the trees
>   Declares a creature new and wild.
>   How many years have I lived this

way?
How many lonely nights have I
consoled myself
With secret places, deep grass, and
powers directly conferred,
By nature herself.
Do I miss the other world –
That world of human companionship,
coffee houses, spring dances,
summer fairs and art museums? Of
marriage and children?
To see this lonely hybrid, this child of
the forest,
Is to see myself. I know him.
Feelings rush back
To haunt my memory. But what to do
about it?

        Pinocchio
What is your name?

        Blue Fairy
My name? Why it is Blue Fairy. But
once, in another life ...

Pinocchio (urging her)
Yes?

Blue Fairy
(she stops herself. Lets go of
memory)
Roll down your pants, time for an
inoculation.

Pinocchio
No way.

Blue Fairy
What do you mean, no way?

Pinocchio
Forget it.

Blue Fairy
But you must: it's a wide-spectrum
antibiotic.

Cricket
Ineffective against fools.

       Pinocchio
Nope. Sorry. Can't do it.

       Blue Fairy
I'll ask you one more time.

       Pinocchio
Stop needling me. Impossible.

       Cricket
Told you. He's a 'fraidy cat. 'Fraid of
needles. 'Fraid of crickets. He's
better off dead.

       Pinocchio
Go take a hike!

       Blue Fairy
A temper as well. Call the
undertakers.

       Pinocchio
Huh?

Suddenly, two human-sized Jack Rabbits enter,
carrying a coffin.

Pinocchio
No way! I'm not going! I've got to find
my father, who gave me my very life
and to whom I owe everything. All he
asked is that I go to school but I've
been distracted lately, you see. And
beaten by ruffians.

Blue Fairy
I suppose they were looking for gold.
You wouldn't happen to have any?

Pinocchio (looking around at the
others, suspicious)
Gold — me? Where would I ever
come by gold?

Pinocchio's nose grows suddenly very long — like
a broom stick.

Pinocchio
What's happening? (Mr. Crow and
Cricket are laughing at him)

Cricket
Never saw a nose lay low when its

owner lies.

Blue Fairy
Perhaps you'd prefer to tell the truth.

Pinocchio (hesitating)
But I did!

Pinocchio's nose grows even longer.

Blue Fairy
You're certain of that?

Pinocchio (conceding defeat)
Ok. Maybe I have one itsy bitsy
piece of gold that I found in a ditch.

Mr. Crow
Undoubtedly fool's gold. And if his
nose is growing, what about his dick!

Blue Fairy
Stop it, Crow. That's disgusting. (To
Pinocchio) Only one, you're quite
sure?

Pinocchio
Definitely only one.

Suddenly his nose grows even longer, extending
the length of the bed he's on, as well as the center
of the bed, which can only confirm Mr. Crow's
erotic insight.

Pinocchio
Well, maybe two pieces.

His nose continues to grow, as do the covers over
his waist. He's definitely taking on a rise.

Pinocchio
Or was it three? Oh hell. Four pieces,
alright? (As he tries to do something
with his omnipresent and
disconcerting lance of a nose and
strange sensation between his legs).

Presently he withdraws his four sovereigns and
shows them to the Blue Fairy.

His nose and erection retreat to more normal size
almost immediately.

Blue Fairy
That's better. (She jabs him in his
hip with the needle and Pinocchio
lets out a pathetic wail)

Pinocchio
Oh I'm hurt! Really badly!

Blue Fairy
That wasn't so difficult. By the way,
you are very singularly built. Your
skin broke the needle.

Cricket
That's because he's made of wood.

Pinocchio
And proud of it. The more I learn
about this world, the more I realize
how precious trees are.
 (To Blue Fairy) By the way, you
should meet my father, Geppetto. I
think you two —

Blue Fairy
Geppetto! (she looks away,

astonished)
I feel weak.
A sensation overtakes me.
Drowning in memory...

She catches herself, then (addressing Pinocchio)
You must stand up!

Pinocchio manages it.

Blue Fairy
There. Can you walk?

Pinocchio
Better yet —

He jumps up and does a pirouette, then dances
with the Three Falcons. The Cricket, aroused by
the rhythm, joins in and plays his own castanets by
simply twitching his antennae.

Blue Fairy (finally catching Pinocchio
in the middle of his dance, clutching
him stolidly so as to listen)
Now listen very carefully. I want you
to go straight home, and watch your

back. No more side roads or
deviations, understand? This is a
test. Tomorrow, after returning the
gold to your Father, you will march
straight to school, study hard, and
then we will see.

Pinocchio
A seat in parliament? A degree in
pharmacology? See what?

Blue Fairy
See about making you a proper boy.

Pinocchio
Is it feasible?

Mr. Crow
Assuming he ever makes it past the
physiological stage of diapered
moron.

Cricket
A menace of exuberance.

First Jack Rabbit
Death warmed over.

Second Jack Rabbit
Pure imagination. Impulse sufficient
to alter the earth's axis, or certainly
change history.

First Falcon
He has more inspiration in his little
finger than all of you combined.

Second Falcon
Ditto that.

First Falcon
You may think him dimwitted, but his
courage is contagious.

Third Falcon
And did you see his fandango?

Blue Fairy
All things are feasible. But it's up to
you, now. Even a lump of wood can
become a butterfly. (and to herself

—) And even a Blue Fairy might yet
find true love.

> Pinocchio (leaping over to kiss her
> on the lips, to the Blue Fairy's
> embarrassment)

Alright then. Here I go!

> Cricket (coming round, generously
> handing him a knapsack with some
> supplies)

Wait — take this. Some rations,
flashlight and pocket-knife. Perhaps
there's hope for you after all.

Act 3
Scene 1

Open countryside. Early morning. Multimedia
video montage over the horizon expands greatly
the various scenes.

> Pinocchio (making his way, stops
> suddenly beneath a large tree and
> low-lying bushes, sees a huge
> python, or cobra)

A serpent! Well then, will you let me
pass or not? For you should know I
am a master at martial arts, Green
Belt, 9th degree, studied under
Steven Seagal, necromancy, voodoo
and puppetry … playing it cool, eh?

The snake is silent and motionless. Pinocchio
throws some absurd punches and judo kicks in the
air, then leaps over the snake, only to land in a
hunter's net. He thrashes about with the pocket-
knife given to him, trying to escape, when
suddenly a carriage filled with children and all of
Geppetto's Marionettes arrives, pulled by
overworked burros.

Medley of Marionettes (from inside
the carriage)
It's that fool, Pinocchio!

Pinocchio
Ms. Rose! Harlequin! Punchinello!
Somebody help me. I'm trapped!

Candlewick jumps from the carriage to rescue him.

Candlewick
Remember me, Candlewick. I saw
you run through the streets of our
village. Nobody knew whether you
were a boy like me or a puppet like
them. But even a half-breed
deserves better than to die in a
hunter's net and eaten by a cobra.

Together, they manage to extricate Pinocchio, who
leaps back on to his feet, brushing himself off.

Pinocchio
Thank you. Most kind, indeed. And
speaking of our village, which way,
please. For I am totally lost. I must

get home to my father as soon as
possible and tomorrow attend my
first day at university. I'm working on
my Aged Pee Dee, You see!

Candlewick
Aged Pee Dee? You mean Ph.D?

Pinocchio
That's the one.

Candlewick
A patently bad idea.

Pinocchio
What do you mean?

Candlewick (to everyone in the
    carriage)
He says he's got to get home so he
can go to school bright and early and
get his Ph.D!

Everyone bursts out laughing with mocking scorn,
with the exception of the burros, who instead are
crying they are so overworked.

Pinocchio
What? Why are you all laughing at
me?

Candlewick
In this economy? Are you kidding?
My cousin got a Ph.D. in Medieval
Studies from Turin University. You
know where that got him?

Pinocchio shakes his head in innocence.

Candlewick
Cleaning toilets at a medieval
monastery in Lombardy, thank you
very much.

Pinocchio
And why are the burros crying like
that?

Candlewick
Don't mind the burros. That's just
their job, to work hard and cry. While
we are all on our way to have eternal
fun in the land of boobies, a perfect

paradise adjoining the sea, where
there is no school, no work, no
politics, no guns, taxes, pollution or
things we have to do. Sleep 'till noon,
leave your dirty socks on the floor,
computer games are free; cell
phones and credit cards too. No
minimum drinking age and almost no
adults to hassle us. Throw in a
mistress or two in Milan, and life is a
dream.

Pinocchio
Come on? Where's the catch?

Medley of marionettes
No catch.
Seize the day.

Candlewick
No harm in trying it out for a few
years.

Pinocchio
How did you find out about it?

Candlewick (looks at the others)
It's one of those secrets people die
for. I can't reveal my source.

Pinocchio
Sounds fishy to me. A few years!
Gynecology class, first thing in the
morning. And then a debate on the
senate floor, and finally, I have to —

Candlewick
No have-to's in Booby Town. And no
guilt, either. And what's this
obsession with school, anyway?
Learn from a book what you'd get
free from life?

Pinocchio
How do you know that, you're only a
kid?

Candlewick

Some kids get around more than others.

Pinocchio

You're sure about this? How many mistresses? By the way, what is a mistress?

Candlewick

As many as you want. They are better than branches filled with leaves in Summer. Grape vines teeming with grapes. Orange trees brimming with oranges. You know what I mean? Succulent, juicy, ripe.

Pinocchio

Well, I know what ripe means. I was a tree, remember.

Candlewick

So there, you see?

Pinocchio

But why is it called Booby Town?

Candlewick (looks at the   others)
You blockhead, 'cause all the girls
have got the biggest boobs there.

  Pinocchio
I don't know.

  Candlewick
What's not to know? And you better
make up your mind because the
burros are getting restless. More so
the Carriage Master, and he is an
adult, and not a very nice one, with
that whip of his. You best mind your
head.

  Pinocchio
Well, tell me one more thing – what
are boobs?

  Candlewick (looking up at the
  heavens with a flabbergasted gasp)
What are boobs? Tits, you idiot.

  Pinocchio (truly innocent)
Tits? Oh ... like titmice, or tomtits?

Beautiful birds. Of course! We had
several that used to nest in —

      Candlewick (ushering him by force)
Just get in for god sakes.

      Pinocchio (as the burros start off
      dragging the carriage, with other
      carriages in the rear)
Well, I suppose the Blue Fairy
wouldn't mind if I just tried it out for a
day or two!

      Candlewick
That's the spirit!

Pinocchio joins the carriage and speaks to one of
the lead burros.

      Candlewick (to the Marionettes)
How does he know how to speak
donkey?

The Marionettes all shrug their shoulders.

Pinocchio
Are you still laughing, or are those
tears from being overworked? If the
latter, I shall certainly have them
ease up, and I have my own rations I
would be only too pleased to share
with you.

Burro
Most kind, Master Pinocchio. But if
the sordid truth be known,
Candlewick and all the others have
made a fatal miscalculation: Booby
Town is actually a colossal booby
trap for blockheads. I should know: I
was one of them!

Carriage Master (whipping the
burros)
Mush!

The carriages, one by one, enter a long dark
tunnel in the heart of a mountain. When they re-
emerge on the other side, revealed to them is a
true childrens' paradise.
Everywhere, around huge campfires, are

chocolate and gumball dispensaries, nudie playing
cards, and children — one naughtier than the next
— playing devilish tricks on each other, all
laughing, screaming, rampaging like little demons.
It is a scene reminiscent — if one were to compare
— of Pieter Breughel's best insanity canvases;
children making fun of the crippled; hunchbacks
begging for a crust of bread while spoiled little
brats throw pies in their faces; girls naughtily lifting
up their skirts; and bullies having one hell of a
time.
All the Marionettes are doing gymnastics,
screeching for no reason, and shouting "Nuke the
babies! Wipe out the adults! Burn down the circus!"

Pinocchio stares in awe, as his carriage
companions leap from their seats to join the fray.

> Carriage Master (tying up the burros,
> to Pinocchio)
> You're part of it now. Enjoy it while it
> lasts! (And he walks away)

> Pinocchio (to the burros)
> What did he mean `While it lasts?'

    Burro
Look over there.

    Pinocchio
What? Look at what?

    Burro
See there, behind it all – those are
ovens.

    Pinocchio
Yes, ovens, where they make all the
chocolate cream pies, lemon tortes,
Christmas cookies, right?

    Second Tethered Burro
Wrong.

    Pinocchio
Wrong? What's wrong with
Christmas cookies?

    First Burro
What he means is, after your first or

second day, they take you away,
throw you in the oven, and cook you
up into something else, whatever
they want you to be – a burro, a
slave, in other words, for life; or,
worse, glue, and sometimes, they
turn a boy into candle wax.

    Pinocchio
That does not set well by me at all.
No, not one bit. And whatever for?
Candle wax?

    Second Burro
To light their way, for their world is
dark indeed.

Now Pinocchio recognizes the place for what it is,
and sees hundreds of poor tethered burros, their
heavy heads hung low, all standing in the mud,
waiting for their next horrible task.

    First Burro
See there? Even the crickets are
forced to work. Indeed, there to the
right is a long line of crickets

dragging a huge tray of chocolate
doughnuts to the Imperial Mansion
atop a rugged cliff.

Second Burro
When they reach the cliff, they turn
the job over to the spiders and the
ants – all indentured – who must
somehow or other get it up to the
Mansion.

Pinocchio
But who's in the mansion?

First Burro
Adults.

Pinocchio
Oh dear. I had a hunch it all sounded
too easy.

But before the horrible revelation fully sinks in,
Candlewick shows up, drags Pinocchio off to a
marshmallow gobbling gang, where Pinocchio can
eat all the toasted marshmallows he likes.

Pinocchio
Not bad. What are they?

Candlewick
Marshmallows. What else would they
be?

Pinocchio
They're pretty good.

Candlewick
PRETTY good. Master Pinocchio,
these are the best marshmallows in
all of Italy.

Pinocchio
I wouldn't know.

Candlewick (recognizing Pinocchio's
          fear)
The facts speak for themselves. I,
too, was skeptical. But there comes
a time in life when we have to believe
in and embrace joy, and not accept
the dreary status quo as our destiny.

This business about going to school,
listening to our parents, earning a
living — it's all mere brainwashing.
They suffered, and expect us to
suffer also.
Well, not me, thank you.
And tomorrow when we wake up, the
proof will be there.

    Pinocchio (agreeing, at least for the
       time being)
Ok. Sure. Why not. Liberation! Hail to
Garibaldi!

    General refrain (everyone tossing
       hats)
Hail to Garibaldi!

Now Candlewick joins some young girls who are
behaving with great promiscuity and binging on
beer. Many others have joined in and the whole
scene reads of Animal House.

    Candlewick (between yawns, emits a
       loud burp, then puts down the jug of
       beer, as others all around him yawn

and burp, one by one passing out
around the campfire)
I feel myself falling off. Very tired.
Very tired ...

Pinocchio
Me too. Good night, Candlewick.

Candlewick
Sweet dreams, sweet dreams ...

All the characters fade into shadow as the
campfire goes out. The moonrise dissolves into
sunrise on the horizon, and with it — the sound of
numerous burros braying. As the stage is further
illuminated, we find ourselves in the heart of Booby
town — brick facades all round, and in the
distance, a wild sea. But now, it appears that all
the children, Pinocchio included, have turned into
Burros, some more than others, and as they
discover this for themselves, one by one, general
pandemonium ensues, marked by lamentations. At
the same time, the skin traders have arrived to bid
at auction on the hides of these doomed animals.

Pinocchio
Oh my God! I knew it!

Auctioneer
Donkey hides, best in the land. What
it will be for this pesky little mule, uh?
I've got a reserve price of five-
thousand Lire. (He beats the donkey
closest to him with a whip) Imagine
the fine shoes he'll make, a
briefcase, or leather jacket.

Pinocchio (to Candlewick, who
cowers beside him)
Hail Garibaldi, my ass! What have
you done. Didn't you know?

Candlewick
If you're so smart, how come you
have the biggest ears in all of Booby
Town?

Pinocchio
Have you looked at *yourself* lately?

Candlewick (feeling his own ears in
horror, crying out)
What are we going to do?

Auctioneer (shouting at Pinocchio)
You! Get over there!

Pinocchio
Not a chance, you little fart-for-
brains! Go pick on somebody your
own size.

The many rough-riding Bidders laugh at the
Auctioneer who attacks and starts to beat
Pinocchio unmercifully.

Auctioneer
I'll show you whose boss!

But Pinocchio, joined by Candlewick, fights back,
but is no match for the three-hundred pound
Auctioneer.

A Skin Merchant
Wait! I like that one's gumption. And
shiny hide. I'll pay seven thousand

Lira. Once I drown him in the sea,
peel back the skin and bake it on
shore, his hide should make an
excellent drum set. My Son wants to
join a rock-and-roll band like U2.
Sign with a record label. And this will
be his Birthday present.

Auctioneer
What a loving father! An example to
us all!

Pinocchio
No! You bastards!

Candlewick (terrified, tries to call out
but can only bray)
….Bray!….

Auctioneer
And good riddance to the trouble-
maker. Sold!

Act 3
Scene 2

The Skin Merchant drags the struggling Pinocchio
to the seashore — a brutal scene — and forces
him down into the water.

> Skin Merchant
> There you go, now die you dumb
> mule!

> Pinocchio (final breaths)
> Oh Geppetto...dear Blue Fairy,
> forgive me....

Suddenly, a huge contraption of a Sea Monster
emerges from the depths of the sea and devours
Pinocchio, his vast razor-sharp set of teeth
narrowly missing the Skin Merchant who has leapt
back, fumbling on his ass onto the higher ground.

The Monster retreats back into the dark depths of
the water.

Pinocchio tumbles down into the far reaches of the
Monster's alimentary canal, filled with strange

objects and a few living creatures, including the
Great White Shark, Sharkey.

Pinocchio
Who are you?

Sharkey
I am Sharkey. Separated from my
school. And you?

Pinocchio
I, too, would be much better off in
school. I thought I knew who I was,
Master Pinocchio by any other name.
Bound for the Roman Senate, the
Billionaire's Club. A red speedster
filled with adoring supermodels. Now
I am mightily confused. I miss the
forest.

Sharkey
Well good luck, my friend, for you are
as far removed from a forest as one
could be.

Pinocchio
So I see.

Sharkey
No point fretting, though. It's just the
way it is.

Pinocchio
You think?

Sharkey
I know.

Sharkey sees that his new friend is not altogether
convinced. Pinocchio is computing volume,
distance, and the stench of stomach enzymes, all
the while figuring out his escape.

Sharkey
What are you doing?

Pinocchio
It's called Philosophy. Soul
searching. I've made some mistakes
in my time.

Sharkey
Yeah, me too. I let two surfers get
away. I just didn't have the heart to
eat them.

Pinocchio
What are surfers?

Sharkey
Food for Great Whites like me. To be
honest with you, I knew there was
one fish bigger than me, or that was
the rumor going around. But nobody
seemed to care and I never met one,
until that fateful day whenever it was,
when I was swallowed like a cup of
tea, and here I am, and here are we.
There's others, by the way, in case
you're curious. Meet The Sadly
Tuna.

Sadly Tuna (lying flat-out on his
belly, big eyes looking around,
lamenting his fate. (Mournfully)
Hello.

Pinocchio
Hello.

Sadly Tuna
You're certainly different.

Sharkey
Yeah, I was noticing the same thing.

Pinocchio
Different? Different how?

Sadly Tuna
Don't know. Can't put my finger on it.
'Course that might be because I
wasn't born with fingers.

Pinocchio
Maybe it's my stubbornness.

Sharkey
That could be it.

Pinocchio
My instincts for survival?

Sadly Tuna
Very likely.

Pinocchio
But most probably it's my stupidity
that has proved the ruin of me.

Sharkey
Now we're talking. But fate also has
a role. After all, I was King of the
Sea, a Great White Shark, as you
can see. Now look at me.

Pinocchio
You're still white?

Sharkey
Thanks.

Sadly Tuna
He didn't even try to eat me. And
we've been crammed next to each
other for days. That's got to say
something about your character.

Sharkey
I appreciate that. I really do. We
sharks are so maligned. Why, for
every nibble I take of a surfer's toe,
one-hundred-ten million of us are
tortured, dismembered, and cut up
into shark fin soup each year so
humans can have something they
don't even like the taste of. Imagine
that. Soon there won't be any Great
Whites left.

Sadly Tuna
Same with us. In fact, every fish I
ever met had a similar tale to tell.
Those humans. No good, if you ask
me.

Pinocchio (totally befuddled)
But it was my hope to become one. A
regular boy. Go to college. Get a
degree. Marry a supermodel and
drive a fancy car.

Sharkey
What are you talking about? You

look like a tree limb to me, with
donkey ears — that's weird — if you
don't mind my saying. It's certainly
not meant as an insult.

Sadly Tuna
He does, come to think of it. A tree
with donkey ears. Very strange.

Pinocchio
It's true. No insult taken.

Sharkey
You see! I knew that, on account of
several hundred million years of
evolution, that and the fact I love to
hang out in forests.

Pinocchio
There are forests in the ocean?

Sharkey
Well, there used to be. Forests of
kelp. Humans are killing those, too,
I'm afraid.

Pinocchio
My goodness, this is all coming as
an awful shock.

Sharkey
Sorry, kid. I didn't mean to spoil your
fun, or dash your dreams, but – well,
look around, this ain't exactly the
Caribbean, if you know what I mean.

Pinocchio
I can't do anything right. Even my
hopes and dreams were all wrong.
And even when I try to do the right
thing, it's useless. It's not that I suffer
from a persecution complex.

Sadly Tuna
Hey, kid, you're a tree, aside from
the ears. You have every right to
suffer a persecution complex.

Pinocchio
I think I suffer because I am who I
am. Or because I've desired that
which is not mine to desire. Or

because, I don't know why, but
maybe I am becoming more human
by the moment.

Sadly Tuna (noticing how
    Pinocchio's donkey ears are
    disappearing)
You certainly are! In fact your ears,
they're ... changing!

Pinocchio (feeling his ears shrinking
    down to human size)
I'm covered in slobber.

Sharkey
Stomach enzymes. They'll eventually
dissolve us into some sort of acid
gob. Not pretty. And nobody will write
about it. Because it's the law of the
sea. Eat and be eaten. No matter
how hard one tries to be kind, it
backfires. I know. I tried to go
vegetarian for nearly seven hours.
Can you imagine!

Pinocchio
And what happened?

Sharkey
A cruise liner, bound from Fort
Lauderdale to the Canaries, must
have been nine stories high, rammed
right into me. Took me a year to
recover. I was too weak to swallow
even a baby shrimp. I lived on
seaweed. I guess that counts as a
vegetarian. Except the parents of the
seaweed were all over me, really
pissed off. 'As if we don't have
enough problems with DDT, and all
sorts of other chemicals; Japanese
connoisseurs, toasting us into paper
— sized filaments that humans eat
like we were crackers or something.
But now a Great White Shark has
taken a liking to seaweed!' And they
all scattered. So you see what I
mean? You can't say I didn't try.

Pinocchio
So we're truly doomed.

Sadly Tuna
I'd have to agree.

Sharkey
Ah get over yourselves. Things could
be worse. At least it'll be a proper
burial, at sea, I mean.

Pinocchio
But I wasn't meant to be buried at
sea?

Sadly Tuna
Bad luck, kid.

Sharkey
Wait a goddamned minute – see
that?

Sadly Tuna
No.

Pinocchio
Yes, the light.

Sharkey
That's not just light, that's a mouth. I
could spot one miles a way. But what
a curious mouth – look there, no
teeth!

Sadly Tuna
He's right. I don't see a single tooth.

Sharkey
Time to get moving. We may have a
chance.
Hold your nose and head for the
light.

Sadly Tuna
And how do you expect me to hold
my nose? I have no hands.

Sharkey
I take it back. Actually, I wasn't going
to say anything, but you stink worse
than all the other stuff combined.
Pinocchio (stroking the Sadly Tuna's
beautiful head)
I'd take that as a compliment.

The three of them make their way up the galley of gastric juices, jetsam and flotsam. The juices melt away the remainder of Pinocchio's donkey ears and tail until he is physically back to his old self. The fish giant's gullet is enormous and filled with drooling stalactites and bits and pieces of flesh and bone. Other elements include various stores from numerous shipwrecked galleons. As they move up the steep gullet towards a sort of plateau where the light is coming from, they hear strange cries in the dark, a cacophony of stranded victims singing their sad dirge.

Sadly Tuna
If I am not mistaken, I hear the sea roar, and the light gets brighter by the second.

Pinocchio surmounts the last hurtle onto the inner digestive plateau and sees someone quietly eating his dinner by lantern light at a little table. Up above, the sea monster's mouth opens and closes rhythmically as the creature sleeps soundly.

Pinocchio (upon coming closer)
Father!

Sharkey
It's a human, and I'm starving. Let
me deal with this!

Geppetto
Pinocchio!

Long-lost embraces, kisses and tears.

Sharkey (to Pinocchio)
You know this human?

Pinocchio
Yes, indeed. Father, how did you
end up in here?

Geppetto
Same as you, I imagine. Searching
for happiness, but now I am certain
my travails were not in vain.

Pinocchio
I was waylaid a hundred times;
beaten up by rogues, accosted right
and left, trapped in a hunter's net and
captured by skin merchants in booby

town. It was terrible!

Geppetto
My poor innocent Pinocchio.
Innocent no longer. But who are
these two? If I'm not mistaken, one is
a tuna and, my Lord, that is a Great
White Shark!

Pinocchio
Don't worry, Dad.

Geppetto
Dad. You called me Dad! Miracolo
dei miracoli.

Pinocchio
This is Sharkey, the only Great White
Shark who ever went vegetarian.

Geppetto
You're kidding? I'd have a hard time
doing it. You know, I'm Italian.

Pinocchio
And this is the Sadly Tuna who,
hopefully, will not be sad much
longer. Sharkey has a plan to get us
out of here.

Geppetto
That would be very good, indeed.
Because I just finished the last of my
food provisions — a can of tuna fish,
no less. My apologies, dear Sir.

Sadly Tuna
Yeah, yeah. I hear that all the time.
(whining —)'But it was dolphin-free
tuna' blah blah blah. Tell that to forty-
eight of my siblings, not to mention
the Blue Fins.

Geppetto
Blue fins?

Sadly Tuna
You've never seen one in your life.
And that's because they're nearly
extinct. Anyway, it's the Atlantic, not

the Adriatic.

      Geppetto (taking his waterlogged hat
      off with sincere contrition)
On behalf of my entire species,
please accept a humble woodcutter's
apology.

      Sadly Tuna
Apology accepted since you're
Pinocchio's Dad. But now you
understand why we are called sadly
tunas.

      Geppetto
I swear, if we get out of here alive, I
shall never ever touch another
morsel of tuna —

      Sadly Tuna
If I had a nickel for every time I heard
that one —

      Geppetto
... or drink even a cup of shark fin
soup — (Sharkey growls, showing off

his ferocious teeth, then says,
"Fintastic!"), or for that matter, I will
never cut another piece of wood as
long as I live.

Pinocchio
But then, Father, how will you live?
Woodcutting is all you know?

Geppetto (Dreamily …)
I've always wanted to do a new
translation of Petrarch's love
sonnets, the old vernacular, into
modern Italian.

Pinocchio
That's the spirit! And I, in turn, vow
that I shall do as I have been
instructed from the start: be a good
boy, go to school, respect all life, and
never hurt a living soul, as the Great
Cricket instructed. No more meat or
fish. Just pasta primavera, raindrops,
and salads with truffles. The diet that
sustained me quite well when I was a
happy piece of wood living in the

forest with my family. (He stops …
remembering back, coming out of
this trance …) My *true* family …

Geppetto
Perhaps I should apologize to you,
as well, Son, for ever having
removed you from that splendid
paradise of yours; that piece of wood
you once were, standing tall in a
sacred grove, no cares at all. It was
my greed that made you.

Sharkey
This is all terribly touching and I don't
mean to break up a moist poignant
Father-Son Come-to-Jesus moment,
but could you two please discuss this
shit once we're out of here?

Geppetto
He's right. I like a practical man.
Pinocchio
He's a shark, Dad.

Geppetto
At this point, a man and a shark are
on the same wavelength. Speaking
of which, it is very wavy out there
and I am very seasick. What do we
do?

Sharkey
This way, Gentlemen, no time for
reminiscing. Hurry! While the
monster still sleeps. Timing is
everything between snores. And
whatever you do, if you need to
vomit, swallow it. Otherwise that's
sure to wake the monster up.

One by one they leap out into the moonlit sea
through the monster's mouth and thus make their
dangerous escape.

Act 3
Scene 3

Back outside Geppetto's hut, the whole village has assembled to welcome the arriving heroes. The Poliziotto, Cricket, Monsieurs Catwell and Foxworth — old, ragged, duly chastised and homeless, Mademoiselle Fire-Eater, Ticket Master, all the Marionettes, even the Cobra, and several burros, among others, are all assembled, for they have heard about Pinocchio and Geppetto's remarkable escape from the sea monster. The news has traveled up and down Italy.

Chorus of Villagers
It's Geppetto, back from the dead.
Welcome! And look who accompanies
him, none other than the little monster
himself, Pinocchio!

Geppetto (kneeling down to kiss the
soil of his own hearth and homeland)
Only someone back from the dead
can truly appreciate hearth and
home.

Ms. Rose (excited to see Pinocchio)
Is it true? A sea monster devoured
you both?

Pinocchio
Yes, Ms. Rose, quite true. But even a
sea monster must sleep from time to
time, affording anyone with a head
on his shoulders the opportunity to
escape. In this case we were
especially lucky. It was such an old
sea monster he had no teeth.

Chorus of villagers (many toasting
jugs of beer to the arriving heroes)
Here here!

Great Cricket (stepping forth with a
cane)
Many adventures, both terrible and
fine; but has he learned the humility
that would transform a foolish
scoundrel into a noble young man?

Pinocchio
Master cricket, old friend. You are

certainly within your right to point out
that I behaved badly in the old days.
By the way, what's with the cane?

Cricket
For us crickets, one year is equal to
a hundred years for a person, or five
hundred for a tree. Winters are
especially challenging. Anything
under 32 degrees Fahrenheit and
we're finished. Meet my children,
Nymph Number One, and Nymph
Number Two.

Pinocchio (bowing)
Nice to meet you. You have a very
learned father. (To Cricket) But
where are their wings?

Cricket
In a few months. Give them time.

Pinocchio
Yes, time. Time plus adversity has
taught me well,
Today a new credo to declare I shall,

That each of us must help old
crickets cross the road.

Cricket
Of what does such humility bode?

Pinocchio (to the burros)
To give assistance to the
overburdened mule,
Could there be a more important
school?
Save a lamb from the skillet,
A piglet from the fire,
Oh that all of us might so aspire.

Geppetto (smiling, nodding, proud)
That's my boy! Is he something! And
guess what: I'm a vegetarian now.

The Chorus of Villagers
Go on! No way!

Geppetto
It's true. Henceforth, no meat for me.

Poliziotto
But fish, surely?

Geppetto
My dear Poliziotto, it was a fish – a
Great White Shark, to be precise,
named Sharkey – who saved our
lives. He'd be with us if he could, but
had a very important appointment far
out at sea. He does send his
regards, however.

As Monsieur Foxworth skulks self-consciously
away from the Village ("no way I'm ever giving up
meat," he hisses), the Cat addresses one and
all —

Catwell
But surely you'd all agree, every law-
abiding Italian is entitled to a little
tuna now and then? Say three times
a day?

Pinocchio
Get out, you good for nothing
scoundrel! I remember you now! He

tied me upside down to a tree!

Monsieur Cat caterwauls and makes to flee, then summons a new plan, and decides, instead to simply apologize.

> Catwell
> I am truly sorry. I was not myself,
> being totally under the influence of
> that miserable wretch, Foxworth.

> Great Cricket (to Pinocchio)
> Verily, you are a new man now.

> Geppetto
> And I, his proud Father, can vouch
> for that. For I owe my life, and my
> soul to this young man.

> Pinocchio
> No, I cannot accept such praise.
> Rather, I celebrate the lonely, sadly
> tuna who now swims freely across
> the seas in search of his own school,
> along with Great White. The two of
> them embody the whole ocean and

all the seas; they showed us the
way, marked the path, struck up the
courage and took the first plunge out
of the mouth of the monster.
Commend the fish – without them,
and the oceans they inhabit, we
would all be dead. I don't claim to
understand the underlying dynamics
because I never finished my Ph.D.,
but I have it on authority that we
need to all be much nicer to one
another, or nobody will make it. And
that includes the lordly burro who
shoulders others' burdens day and
night. For what, a few pinches of
straw, filthy wasp-infested water
holes, and incessant beatings?
(Pinocchio hugs the mule standing
nearby).
Commend the wise old cricket, who
helps put us all to sleep at night
without the need of Valium.
Give thanks to the rain. The snow.
The birds and the bees. They are the
true philosophers of the
world.Unnoticed by the other

villagers amid the fanfare, Two Jack
Rabbits, Mr. Crow, and the Three
Falcons all arrive in the rear of the
gathering.

Geppetto
You are a good son, a great son,
because you have dreamt that it was
possible, and struggled to be one,
against all odds. Like a flying fish
who transcends, even for a fleeting
instant, every limitation imposed
upon him by nature.
I only wish that this old man could
have provided you with a loving
mother.
For it takes a woman to consummate
creation; a woman to shape true
destiny and make it whole.
Once I loved such a woman, but
alas, she is long gone.

Pinocchio (seeing the Rabbits,
Falcons and Mr. Crow)
Have faith, Father.

Poliziotto
Spring is coming, Geppetto. Plenty of
trees for you to cut.

Geppetto
No, no more cutting of trees.

Poliziotto
No meat, no fish, and no trees? You
will starve. What, you will eat
crickets?

Cricket
I beg your pardon?

Geppetto
I told you. I am a vegetarian from
now on. That includes insects. I will
nibble on moonbeams and sleep in
beds of grass. And when the odd
guava or coconut falls to the ground,
after the squirrels have had their
taste, and the hummingbirds, as well,
then I shall have my dinner on what
remains.

Mr. Crow
Um, I hate to be the harbinger of bad
news but, this is Italy. I'd know if
there were guavas or coconuts.

Pinocchio
He's going to translate Petrarch's
love sonnets into a modern idiom.

Geppetto (humbly)
For young lovers, of course.

Poliziotto
Since when is a woodcutter a poet?

Geppetto (fondly remembering)
I was not always a crude killer of
wood. Once, when I was a young
man, I lived, I drank, I survived only
on poetry. I was a Romantic living in
a loft near the Uffizi. I worshipped
Dante. Raphael. Leonardo. Who
doesn't when they're young!

Poliziotto
Yes, but now you're old, tired, poor.

Suddenly a fantastic eerie blue light begins to rise from the horizon and cast its enchantment over the entire village.

> Pinocchio (the first to recognize her)
> Father, look!

The Blue Fairy is descending from the top of the theatre on scarcely visible wires, aflame in azure magnificence.

> Blue Fairy
> Dear Geppetto! Do you remember me?

> Geppetto (peering astonished at her)
> Pinocchia! Is it really you?

> Blue Fairy (aka Pinocchia)
> I still see the very day I wandered away into those woods yonder. A storm brewed. The winds carried my own dreams far off into strange lands, through high meadows and into deep forest. There I stayed, a wild child, half-a-lifetime ago. Free to

be myself.

Geppetto
But nobody ever found you? We
thought you were dead. A wolf, a
bear, a viper. Or a drowning. My one
and only true love, shattered.

Blue Fairy
You never gave the slightest
indication of your feelings?

Geppetto
I know.

Blue Fairy
I was neither dead nor alive, but filled
with new powers. The solace of ants,
a cricket, a crow and a bear. And
then arrived this wounded wondrous
personage named Pinocchio
spouting all sorts of surrealities,
including a name,

Geppetto.
And it all came back to me in a flash.

My village. My earlier life. My true
love, you Geppetto.

Geppetto
Me? (to the villagers) Did you all hear
that? Me! A poor good-for-nothing
woodcutter.

Blue Fairy
And from that moment, the path
home appeared clear.

Geppetto (taking hold of her hand)
The boy needs a mother.

Blue Fairy
The mother needs a husband.

Geppetto
The husband can think of no greater
joy! (he takes her in his arms and
they hug gratefully and lovingly)

Cricket
Now there can be no doubt about it:
Pinocchio is really a boy, a person,

just like a human, for he is crying.

All embrace and celebrate, singing a final hymn (or
what the audience would expect to be the final
closing hymn).

> Chorus of Villagers
> (including all the Marionettes,
> Poliziotto, Cricket and Nymphs,
> Catwell, Foxworth who has returned,
> never one to miss a celebration,
> Mr. Crow, Rabbits, Falcons,
> Geppetto and Blue Fairy). But
> Pinocchio does not sing, standing,
> rather to the side, and drifting further
> and further to the side as the hymn
> is sung.

"From a crude dumb stump of wood,
the life of a nobleman has arrived
home, in a village that welcomes
him, his father, and long lost
Pinocchia. God is wonderful. Life is
beautiful. We all must love one
another. No more grief. No more
jealousy or rage. Share our food
together, kill no living being. Live in

peace. And no more Italian politics.
No more grief. No more killing. Live
in peace. We all agree. Bless you,
Lord. For you have given us the
courage of our long-suppressed
convictions."

Everybody hugs. Then —

> Blue Fairy
> Pinocchio, you're not singing. I think I
> know why.

> Geppetto
> Son, what's wrong.

> Pinocchio
> Father, forgive me. It was your
> natural curiosity to bring something
> into being. Imagination is also
> sacred, and I should not have traded
> this new me for a million trees. That
> was then. But this is now. And a
> million trees are everything to me.
> Everything to this village, to Italy, to
> the world.

Geppetto
What are you saying?

Blue Fairy
I know exactly what he's saying.

Cricket
Yes.

Mr. Crow
Of course.

Three Falcons and Two Rabbits (in
    unison)
It's only natural.

Geppetto
What?

Pinocchio (extending his hands to
    those of old Geppetto. Not hugging
    him, but holding his hands,
    somewhat distanced)
Dear Man, friend, person: Thank you,
from the bottom of my heart. But, like
Sharkey and the Sadly Tuna, I have

a different destiny.

Geppetto (wiping away his tears)
But how will you find your way back
to the forest, your true home, your
true family?

Poliziotto (also crying)
I'm sorry I ever arrested him.

Geppetto
How will I live without him?

Cricket
Good-bye dear friend.

Pinocchia (Blue Fairy)
He'll know the way. It's inside him.
Just as I knew the way home, to you
Geppetto.

A final embrace, as Pinocchio bids farewell and
walks off set amid a wonderful Spring wind that
tosses colorful leaves in every direction on stage.

Finito.

Afterword

Everything is as it appears, and nothing is. Every work of the imagination holds itself hostage but may engender all possible contexts for reinventing those alluring exits which do not otherwise exist but in our free reign of fantasy. A tree is a tree is a tree. Yes. But it is also a real tree! A poet has roots, as well, and, in the case of the author of "Pinocchio," those taproots lay claim to a vast fortune of historic details. Some might call them minutia, trivia, while yet others will obtain vestiges, even the vague hint of a glimpse, a horizon line, a tortured look-alike knot in the forest that helps explain so much, so many heretofore unexamined markings in the sand, ancient carvings into the bark.

There is the man Enrico Mazzanti, a 19th century engineer who would turn to cartoons to quench an otherwise indecipherable yearning. What gave him to indulge this conception of the most famous puppet in the world? His image of Pinocchio graces the cover of this Libretto, as it did the original aggregated book by one military volunteer, Carlo Lorenzini (1826-1890) who would take up arms in the Italian movement for unification in the mid-19th century, a War of Independence in 1848 that aspired to see Giuseppe Mazzini and others of the Risorgimento, among them Giuseppe Garibaldi and Victor Emmanuel II, help bring down the existing leadership. Lorenzini's "Il Lampioni," a daily newspaper he created, meant to aid Italy's political turns of fortune through political satire, was a short-lived endeavor, shut down with the rise of the Grand Duke Leoopold who did not take kindly to such criticism. This politically-inclined skeptic, Lorenzini, a hard-nosed journalist, soldier of fortune was thus waylaid mid-course by the last thing on earth he was expecting: to translate children's stories for a publisher in his home town of Florence. Despite his writing two scarcely-received novels ("Un romanzo in vapore" and "Il viaggio per l'Italia di Giannettino") he had probably given up on the idea of a Lorenzini breaking into that rarified realm of great literature. Or had he decided on a course of heresy? (The aftermath of this little saga would suggest that to be the case – but real life does not anticipate such hindsight). In either case, whatever the real motive, he was about to change the course of history.

By 1860, he was using his pen-name, Collodi (the name of his mother's village). What was he thinking? Did he have the slightest inkling of what was to come?

It was the year 1875 when the small publisher in Florence specializing in children's materials, Felice Paggi, suggested to this linguistically-adept would-be captain of the brigades, and former political commentator, that he take Charles Perrault's "Mother Goose" and turn it into proper Italian. For an intellectual who followed every hysterical outbreak of philosophy; each turnabout in the politics of the day, this commission might have come as a profound let down, even an embarrassment. He needed to work, that much is always clear. But "Mother Goose" was no Marxist treatise; nothing like the subtle masterpieces produced by so many of those great names populating his native Tuscany. This was a plump, dead-end schoolbook mentality beset by simple fables, an absence of the slightest nuance or controversy, thoroughly inoffensive standard fare.

Looking more deeply, as he obviously did, Charles Perrault (1628-1703), whose Mother Goose Collodi was now instructed to translate, did not lack for complexity. The author of Little Red Riding Hood, of Sleeping Beauty, Puss in Boots, Bluebeard and Donkeyskin, among others, had firmly established the dark undersides of childhood. It was not Perrault's subtlety that interested the schoolmarms and librarians of late 19th century Italy. But it clearly interested and helped form Collodi.

Within six years, Collodi had found his true vein as an author and by July 7th, 1881, the many memorable creatures of his Storia di un Burattino (Tale of a Puppet) were ready to be launched in a magazine devoted specifically for children, the "Giornale per i bambini".

There is an anecdote – it may be true, or not – that Collodi was unconvinced about the quality of his tale of a puppet and told the publisher that it was a "childish piece" and only hoped that – were the enterprise to move forward, that Collodi be paid sufficiently so as to incite him to continue with the concept, the characters, the story line. By all appearances the story was not unappreciated and by 1883 Collodi had finished, and Felice Paggi had published the entire novel. Dying suddenly in Florence in 1890, one month shy of the age of 64, Lorenzini would never know that his little puppet would enjoy hundreds of editions, translations into over 260 languages and dialects, whole industries created around him, the entire literary world changed forever. Typical.

Considering who jumps up and down and runs circles around the world, those myriad dramatic personae of Collodi's tale, we all may one day look back at Pinocchio and recognize ourselves in this Tuscan mirror; gaze directly upon the tragic-comedy of the human saga; the insanity of a biological crisis we have unleashed in the name of ourselves; for the sake of our children, and their children. Curiously, Collodi questions childhood in an ambiguous manner, suggesting that their indifference, at times, to the health of the Earth; their stubborn refusal to obey rules, to step into line, to be good little boys and girls, may be the salvation, or the destruction we see everywhere around us in the 21st century. Indeed, Pinocchio is ready to squash the cricket, and there is plenty of evidence within the tale to indicate ill-boding currents that go far more than merely implicating the lie. Collodi suggests, as Orwell would in Animal Farm, that power is not merely vested in humanity, but in Nature herself, though it is humanity that most easily abuses its privileges.

All that, in addition to being delightful! Hence, a psychological thriller that prefers the joy of discovery to the dark corridors of what is actually going on. But they are not mutually exclusive and what Lorenzini did by joining them was, obviously, a masterful way to unlock that which had been kept secret, far off in a dark forest of his ancestral landscapes. It started there in Tuscany, birthplace not only of the Lorenzinis, but also of Dante and Botticelli, Leonardo da Vinci and Galileo, Petrarch and Vespucci. The great Puccini hailed from this region where the local word, pinolo, or pignolia, referring to the native pine nut, has everything to do with Pinocchio, and the origins of this particular adaptation. Tuscany is to Italy, what Burgundy is to France – biologically and artistically.

Of the nearly 125 species of pine worldwide (molecular biologists and botanists debate the precise number, of course), about 20 of them produce edible seeds, or nuts. The predominant European pine nut comes from the Stone Pine *(Pinus pinea),* and in Tuscany for some six millennia it has been cultivated. Neanderthals probably harvested it from wild trees, the original members of the Pinaceae family. In the Old Testament, Hosea 14:8, there is a green fir tree mentioned and scholars recognize in it a fruit that was probably the same Stone Pine nut found in many parts of Europe, not just Italy. The tree was worshipped by the Greeks because it was sacred to the God Neptune. Not only were pine nuts found in the rubble after 79 A.D., when Mount Vesuvius blew her stack, but it was a common staple for the Roman Legions wherever they roamed. In fact, these pine nuts were probably the preeminent European snack, going back as far as you care to look. And for nutritional benefits, beauty, and tenacity, the Italian Stone Pine is considered among the most steadfast and loyal of pine trees in the world.

Loyal, you ask? A tree that is loyal?

My version of Pinocchio is born of such a tree.

Along comes a chemist, environmentalist and justifiably proud historian of his native Tuscany, Professor Ugo Bardi from the Dipartimento di Chimica at the Università di Firenzi, who declares, "Plant trees, disband the army, work together: the Tuscan way of surviving collapse."(n.1) What is he referring to? Jared Diamond's "Collapse"? Collapse in general? In fact, writing his essay as recently as 2006, he is speaking of the current dependency on foreign oil and the spate of ecological problems that have historically affected this remarkable region of Italy, Tuscany. He is certainly drawing graphic conclusions from Gibbon's "Decline and Fall of the Roman Empire", and from such examples of twenty-two civilizations described by the late historian Arnold Toynbee, cultures that vanished because they violated their most important compact, namely, a respect for wilderness and ecological carrying capacity. Instead, these cultures, one by one, succumbed to the same gruesome syndrome of self-destruction by which the soils were destroyed, the trees cut down, every last precious mineral extracted, rivers fouled, fisheries, docile birds, anything that moved within striking distance, decimated.

For Professor Bardi, Tuscany, birthplace of Pinocchio, is a fitting metaphor for what continues to happen across the planet. Bardi examines the over-exploitation of the soil by the Roman Empire, later waves of deforestation that filled the Tiberis River with silt, consequent famines that erupted, and the first European waves of environmental refugees. With the final implosion of the once vast Roman military hegemony, Tuscany was liberated in the sense that it could breathe freely again, her soils regenerating critical nutrients, and ecosystems returning to some level of stability.

But by the time of the early Italian Renaissance, there was more industrialization, a repeat scenario of centuries before; Pisa's port was filled with silt from all the new erosion that came with the cutting down of second and third growth trees. Commerce coincided with the production of charcoal used in the making of fire-arms; these weapons in turn argued for their use. And used they were: in battle after battle, as adjoining territories teeming with warriors took up arms, power struggles ensued, and life was again imperiled. The history of Europe.

In the 1520s the leadership of the Republic of Florence, cognizant of approaching adversaries, the Spanish Imperial Armies heading directly towards Tuscany, built enormous fortresses. Michelangelo was one of many locals who found himself frantically trying to buffer frescoes and church domes by covering them with blankets, or building up whole mattresses in an effort, mostly futile, to protect church art from the invaders.

Conditions became so dreadful that it is rumored by the late 16th century, bread not even suitable for hungry dogs was the staple diet in Tuscany, an area once rich in every respect, that had become one of the poorest, depauperate regions in all of Europe. Imagine, a region of some nearly 9,000 square miles in the heart of Italy, its capital being Florence; that biocultural hub that gave birth to such ancient cultures as the Villanovans, the Etruscans, and to the very Renaissance itself, reduced to rubble and squalor.

With little else to sustain the remaining inhabitants, ancient (obviously organic) agricultural techniques were again embraced to try and revivify a dying culture and in this effort the revered Tuscan Saint Giovanni Gualberto (995-1073), known for having gotten out and planted trees his entire adult life, was recalled with urgent fondness. Duke Ferdinando 1st embraced Gualberto's creed to bring his country back to the living. The Duke's symbol become one of "working bees" – producing life-affirming fruits of the land. The strategy succeeded.

Meanwhile, Jews fleeing from the Spanish Inquisition were welcomed in Tuscany; the death penalty and all forms of torture were abolished, Tuscany becoming the first government body to achieve these humanitarian ends anywhere in the world. And today, as Professor Bardi notes, Tuscany has more forest than virtually any other region of Italy. This ecological renaissance is based upon a rural love affair, the endless embrace of nature, as recounted in every art form, love sonnet, that evanescent landscape behind "The Mona Lisa" or "Virgin of the Rocks." An impression easily obtained by visiting the little sequestered village in the hills after whom the author of Pinocchio adopted his nom de plume, the village of Collodi where Lorenzini's mother worked as a maid for the richest family in town, the Garzonis. They would, in turn, honor that woman and her son who today Italy knows to be one of the great literary geniuses of all time.

The town of Collodi, founded in the late 1100s, is described by many as being in perfect harmony with its surroundings. Atop the town, with steps leading to it, is found the great Church of Saint Bartolomeo. Bartolomeo was the son of a ploughman, one of the Twelve Apostles of Jesus who- according to Saint Jerome- carried a copy of the Gospel all the way to India. At the base of the village are the magnificent Baroque gardens of the Villa Garzoni, along with the wonderful park designed by Ottaviano Diodati in the 18th century, said to be the most sublime of all parks in Italy and dedicated to the memory of Pinocchio. The Garzoni gardens spread out along flirtatious grids adrift in whimsy, mythic statues, follies, caves, aviaries, a butterfly house with Lepidoptera species from ecosystems all over the world. A place for fantasies that even includes the so-called "fairytale road" that leads meanderers from Collodi to the nearby town of Pescia, over hillsides where wanderers can daydream in their own stride. A pathway like that to the Land of Oz, or Through a Looking Glass, with works of art interspersed between streams, deep forests, a monastery, and mysterious diversions.

And along the very fortress that Michelangelo helped protect, is the Porte Sante, a cemetery designed in 1854 that holds the body of Carlo "Collodi" Lorenzini, in addition to other poets, sculptors, painters, filmmakers and notable individuals of the region.

An Italian national organization devoted to Collodi's genius (The Fondazione Carlo Collodi) has amalgamated an inventory of the astounding proliferation of translations, adaptations, illustrations, imaginative by-products, sequels, and interpretations of Pinocchio from 1883 to the present. It is a formidable legacy encompassing video games and comic books, plays, musicals, toys, memorabilia, animation of every sort; movies, television series, and countless language editions. Pinocchio has breathed life into thousands of subsequent renditions and works of art indebted to this remarkable creation.

From an "Astro Boy" in Japan, Stephen Speilberg's film "AI – Artificial Intelligence," rapper and jazz saxophonist renditions (including a piece by Wayne Shorter recorded on a Miles Davis album), to Mickey Rooney and much later, Roberto Benigni and Pee Wee Herman all playing the title role of Pinocchio, to the opera by Jonathan Dove at the Great Theatre in

Leeds in 2007, the legend lives on. Danny Kaye and Martin Landau both played Geppetto; Julia Louis-Dreyfus (of "Seinfeld" fame) once played the Blue Fairy.

There have been Pinocchio's in Africa and in outer space; in paintings by contemporary artists like Jim Dine, and in philosophical embraces like those of the rigorous Italian thinker Benedetto Croce (1866-1952) who considered "The Adventures of Pinocchio" a fine example of his "absolute idealism," a notion that aesthetics is core to all philosophy.

In the 1940 Walt Disney Animated Classics version (the second of such films following upon "Snow White and the Seven Dwarfs") Pinocchio's voice was performed by Dickie Jones, Jiminy Cricket by Cliff Edwards and Geppetto by Christian Rub. The storyboards for that production remain classics. But the myriad illustrators in the last nearly 130 years –from Attilio Mussino and Giovanni Manca to Walt Disney's own Pinocchio illustrator, Swedish-born Gustaf Adolf Tenggren (1896-1970) are far too diverse to catalogue, in a league with the illustrations of "Don Quixote". In fact, in 1937 there were an estimated 80 simultaneous editions being published of Pinocchio, just that year, almost all of them illustrated.(n.2)

What I will tell you is that Pinocchio's "Adventures" in this Libretto have been re-examined in light of Tuscany's history, and the current state of the world. Such that, I wosuld add that I have sought to give Collodi's Pinocchio his own dignity, his roots, to take him back to the original landscape where he was born, both as an ideal, but also as a reality in a world where trees, let alone pine nuts, are disappearing rapidly. As if to say: be what you are, and if that happens to be a tree, how fortunate for all concerned.

Fortunately for Tuscany, and for the legacy of Collodi, the Tuscan countryside has been much revived following World War II. There are six UNESCO World Heritage sites (including Florence, Siena and the Cathedral of Pisa); and over 120 nature and scientific reserves. But with over 10 million tourists per year, pressures on Tuscany's biological heritage are not diminishing. Throughout Italy, 547 birds have been identified, many in Tuscany (no endemic birds in Italy, or anywhere in Europe, but a breeding ground, a place of hospice for migratory birds that annually move from the far Northern Boreal forests to the Mediterranean or parts of Africa). Naturalist Damiano Andreini refers to thousands of species found in the Tuscan marshes, including the Trifid Bur Marigold *(Bidens tripartite),* the Nonnotto Botarus Stellaris or Bittern, the Ragno d'Acqua or common pond skater (Gerris lacustris) as well as many other remarkable creatures, many with peculiar, little known indigenous names, where science and literature were made for each other. (n.3)

In a recent study focusing on a biodiversity revival program called Re.Na.To., 88 habitats and 472 plant species were identified within Tuscany as suffering from various degrees of threat and vulnerability.(n.4) Among Italy's many tree species, the predominant ones – such as the holly or Holm oak, the pine (including Aleppo, maritime and umbrella pines in addition to the more common above referenced Italian Stone pine) – are all in need of the same Tuscan protective umbrella that was first manifested by Saint Giovanni Gualberto, (n.5) a passion for nature that culminated, of course in the works of Fra Angelico, Leonardo, Raphael, the later Italian landscapists, not to mention the remarkable life of Saint Francis.

There is much work to be done to maintain protection of this precious historical, ecological and artistic center of the world. Pinocchio is one of those charter members, a veritable signatory to a

Declaration of Biological Rights; not only of the plant community in his native land, but of humanity's future place in a world at risk, where common sense, imagination, an unstinting love of life, not to mention a sense of humor are worth their weight – not in gold – but in old forest, healthy soils, rich biomass, a dazzling, unchallenged array of plant and animal life, clean air and plenty of fresh water to drink. These are, after all, the real concerns of any pine nut, let alone the Pinocchio kind.

Michael Charles Tobias

Footnotes

1. See "Transition Culture – 11 Dec 2006,"?"Plant trees, disband the army, work together: the Tuscan way of surviving collapse" by Ugo Bardi, at: http://transitionculture.org/2006/12/11/plant-trees-d isband-the-army-work-together-the-tuscan-way-of-surviving-collapse-by-ugo-bardi/

2. See JSTOR, "Centenary of a Character: Pinocchio," by Angela M. Jeannet, Italica, Vol. 59, No. 3, Pedagogy (Autumn, 1982), pp. 184-186, Published by: American Association of Teachers of Italian, URL: http://www.jstor.org/stable/478984?© 1982 American Association of Teachers of Italian; See also the "Infography about Pinocchio," http://www.infography.com/content/927376398317. html

3. "Wetlands: The Flora and the Fauna of the Marshlands of Tuscany," by Damiano Andreini, at: http://www.slowtuscany.it/tuscany/pistoia-prato/We tlands.htm

4. See "The Protection Of Biodiversity in Tuscany," by Paolo Emilio Tomei and Andrea Bertacchi,

Department of Agronomy and Agroecosystem Management, Università degli Studi di Pisa, in the book, Nature Conservation: Concepts and Practice, ed. By Dr. Dan Gafta and Dr.John Akeroyd, Spinger Berlin Heidelberg, 2006.

5. See "Plants of Italy: Discover the Mediterranean Trees and Herbs Found in Italy," by Sharon Falsetto, on Suite 101, March 20, 2009, http://www.plant-ecology.suite101.com/article.cfm/plants_of_italy

About Michael Charles Tobias

Michael Charles Tobias is the author of 45 books and several hundred essays, in addition to having written, directed and produced nearly 150 films. An ecologist, mountaineer, explorer, anthropologist and historian, his field research has taken him to some 80 countries where his passion for animal liberation, non-violence activism and zoosemiotic cybernetics, has resulted in his uniquely quirky approach to what he calls "pragmatic idealism" – in the tradition of Parmenides, Ovid, Cervantes, Milton, Shelley, Joyce, Hugh Lofting, Jean-Paul Sartre and Samuel Beckett.

His recently published novel *Professor Parrot and the Secret of the Blue Cupboard* is very much a sequel to Tobias' 1836-page illustrated epic, *The Adventures of Mr. Marigold.* Tobias lives with his life-long partner and wife, the ecologist, author, filmmaker and philanthropist, Jane Gray Morrison.

For more works written by Michael Tobias and published by Zorba Press, please visit this web page: http://www.zorbapress.com/?page_id=106

About Zorba Press

Zorba Press is an independent publisher of books, multimedia books and audio books (forthcoming), and user-friendly ebooks in many formats. From the gorgeous gorges of Ithaca, New York, we publish the paperback books *The Zorba Anthology of Love Stories; The Ithaca Manual of Style;* the anthology *Zenlightenment!;* and a wild comic novel about love and eros (for adults) *Thoreau Bound: A Utopian Romance in the Isles of Greece.*

Currently, we offer about 30 titles – fiction and non-fiction. Recent publications include *The Terrestrial Gospel of Nikos Kazantzakis* by Thanasis Maskaleris; and *50 Benefits of Ebooks: A Thinking Person's Guide to the Digital Reading Revolution.* We publish a number of wonderful novels by Michael Tobias in paperback; and the first ebook edition of a modern classic, Tobias's extraordinary novel, *The Adventures of Mr Marigold.*

Zorba's mission is to promote the innovative ideas and the daring books that nourish children and childhood, point the way to a culture of non-violence, create a sustainable future, and nurture – for every living being – a new world of love, kindness, courage, creativity, sincerity, and peace.